A LAKE HOUSE HOLIDAY

MEGAN SQUIRES

To Brad.

Your unending support means more
than I could ever fit into a few sentences here.
You encourage me to run after my dreams and to live up to the
faith you have in me, and for that,
I'm so very grateful.

I love you always.

1

JOLENE

ACE BARKED THREE times every morning, right at the stroke of seven.

He was the best alarm clock Jolene Carter ever had, but he didn't appreciate it when she'd bop him squarely on his head in an attempt to hit the snooze, like she did that morning. He let his distaste be known with a low rumble in his throat. It would've intimidated a stranger, but little about the one-hundred-pound ball of fluff could rattle Jolene.

The dog had wandered his way out of the dense Merrylark forest line and onto Jolene's property years ago, and after posting on local websites and venturing a trip down the hill to the humane society, she concluded that the mutt had been abandoned on purpose. That revelation broke Jolene's heart, yet at the same time healed it. Ace could become rightfully hers.

And they needed each other. How they needed each other.

They'd been a team for four years now, but judging from Ace's annoyed groan, he wasn't as thrilled about the ongoing partnership.

"Oh, cheer up, grumpster," Jolene teased as she rolled over to rough up the soft hair of his hackles. "I'm only trying to get a rise out of you. You make it so easy."

Ace groaned again and stretched his long body out on the mattress, his paws shoving down the flannel sheets to the foot of the bed, bunching them up like an accordion.

"I wouldn't bop you if you could just find a different way to wake me up, you know," she reasoned with the animal. "Barking is so loud. Startles me every single morning. Maybe a lick on the cheek or a nuzzle under my chin instead?" On cue, Ace rolled onto his back to face her. He pressed a soft paw to her collarbone. His chestnut eyes blinked twice, then stayed shut as he drifted back to sleep, his wakeup call duties complete. "Silly pup."

Swinging her legs over the side of the bed, Jolene paused to let the sleep lift from her eyes. Gold streaks of winter morning light slanted through the window in front of her, hitting her toes as they painted the worn and knotty hardwood. Through the window frame, waves crested and fell across the lake. They looked like thousands of tiny mirrors in mosaic form as they caught the glimmering winter sunlight. It was a new, original piece of artwork every morning, and Jolene treasured that daily gift.

Her heart swelled along with the waves.

"Coffee?" She turned to Ace as he let out a huff. "I'll make yours extra caffeinated. Sounds like *someone* needs it this morning."

The closet was a short walk from the bed and she padded across the room to collect her fuzzy robe and slippers. Even though the day's temperatures promised to be warmer than yesterday's, mornings always began with a chill that caused Jolene to tug the sash on her robe just a little tighter to keep in the extra body heat. She liked days like that, ones that swung all over the thermometer.

Making her way to the kitchen, she flipped the switch to the coffee maker on the counter and it roared to life. Within minutes, the entire house awoke with the invigorating scent of rich, dark coffee. Jolene pulled her favorite Christmas mug from the sink, rinsed it quickly, and poured the drink all the way to the rim. Even though the holiday was still weeks off, she had already packed away her everyday plates, dishes, and bowls and restocked her cabinets with festive and colorful serveware boasting illustrated evergreen trees and holly berries on their surfaces.

Jolene took a swig of the coffee, a spicy blend with notes of nutmeg. The first sip was always her favorite. She warned herself each time that it would be too hot and cause her taste buds to sizzle right off, but she never could help herself from stealing that initial guzzle before the temperature had sufficient time to cool. Jolene wasn't very good at waiting on things.

Glancing out the back window, she saw the familiar shadow of her deck rocker swaying. With a mug in one hand, she retrieved and filled another and then walked to the back door of the house. Roger Wilkins looked up as Jolene stepped across the threshold and onto the back deck. His wire spectacles were low on his bulbous, red nose and needed the push of his index finger to slide them back up the bridge where they belonged.

"Morning, Jojo." Tremors in his hands shook as he stretched out to collect the proffered cup. "Glorious day."

"Indeed," Jolene agreed as she took her usual place beside him. "Coffee's hot. Careful."

"I sure hope you're not worried I'll sue over scalded taste buds. Don't have much need for them anymore and certainly don't have much need for any of your money, either."

She laughed. "That's awfully good to hear because I don't have any to offer."

"No, no," he said, his head nodding in a constant and wobbly bob. "But money's not always the most valuable thing a person can have."

"Starting in with the words of wisdom already? I need at least one cup before I can process anything, remember? At the very minimum, a few sips." Her rosebud lips pressed to the mug and she slurped in a mouthful that had cooled to a drinkable temperature. She could hear Roger laugh at her side, his crackly chuckle a comforting sound.

They sat in companionable silence for a long stretch of time. Jolene always enjoyed watching the winter forest awake across the expanse of water—the way the deer would prance in and out of the stalks of trees and how the birds would flutter about, ready to get the worm with an eagerness only Mother Nature could bring forth in the wintery temperatures.

From his seat next to her on the deck, Roger mouthed the verses in his Bible while he read, and every once in a while his volume would increase and the sounds would become an audible murmuring. Jolene loved it. It was as though he was reading his devotional to her, including her in the spiritual routine like he was the pastor and she, the congregation.

He shut his book after several minutes and looked up. "Big plans today?"

Jolene's mug had run dry so she settled it onto the small table between them. There was already a stained ring on the hardwood top and she fit the empty cup within its circular loop. "Just the holiday craft fair later this morning. I told Cat

I'd help with the coffee truck since Vick's gone down the hill for Tanner's hockey tournament. Shouldn't be too long. Just a couple of hours. She's always so short staffed for these sorts of things."

"I sure hope you're not volunteering again." Roger looked sideways at his young friend through low glasses. They never could seem to stay put where they belonged on his narrow face. Jolene didn't answer. "Jojo, dear, you need to stop doing favors for everyone around here. First the O'Connells use you as their own personal house maid and now you're making mochas for free for the Feltons? You gotta start charging what your helping hand is worth, sweetheart, or you'll be taken advantage of 'til kingdom come. Your generosity needs to be appreciated."

"It's not being taken advantage of if you offer your help freely. You know I like keeping up the O'Connell place. Plus, they pay me enough to make ends meet. And Cat's got more on her plate than she can handle right now. I'm more than happy to help ease their burden. No sweat off my brow. I like helping my friends succeed."

"You can ease their burden without being a burden to their pocketbook, you know. Their success means they can *afford* to pay you. You think Scott McKinley's making cappuccinos for free? No ma'am. Guarantee he's demanding a wage that's more than fair. And the O'Connells have more money than they know what to do with. It's why they're able to maintain a guest house at a lake that they haven't even seen in over five years."

"Well, in fairness, I maintain it."

"My point exactly." Roger's frail hand came down over Jolene's. His skin was like crepe paper, soft to the touch. She wondered what his hands must've been like in his youth when they held strength and vigor and roughness born from work. At one point in time, she figured he'd had hands young women competed with one another to hold. "Can't live off of the savings forever, Jojo. You and I both know that, hard as it is to hear."

Roger wasn't trying to upset her, of course not, but she felt her green eyes burning and she blinked them swiftly to halt whatever emotion was tempted to come out. They had an awful habit of spilling over without her permission. "Another cup?"

Her old friend sighed. "One's all I can handle. Already got the shakes bad enough without the added help of caffeine." Roger smiled sweetly and rocked back in his chair, his rust-colored loafers planted on the splintered decking to keep steady. "I need to head down the hill to the post office this morning, but Millie said she'd let me take her to the fair, so I just might see you there when you're working Cat's coffee truck."

"*Volunteering.*"

As Roger rose slowly from his seat, his back hunching and legs protesting against the strenuous effort, he shook his head, swinging it side to side. His glasses fell off and clattered to the wooden boards. "Stubborn thing, you are, dear."

"I love you too, Roger." Jolene collected her mug and his glasses and stood from the rocker, though she kept her motions purposefully slowed. Roger had been known to call her a showoff a time or two when she outdid him.

"And I, you, Jojo. And I, you."

❋

"DECAF, PEPPERMINT WHITE mocha!"

"Thanks, Scotty!" Jolene grabbed the pink paper cup and slid it into a folded cardboard sleeve.

Things slowed as fairgoers transitioned over to Santa's Workshop set up at the far end of the street. During the winter months, downtown Merrylark became a wonderland of brilliant holiday lights, all sparkling and twinkling in time with familiar carols that echoed through rented sound systems. Though Christmas was still three weeks off, Merrylark was ready for it, the festivities underway.

After handing the customer her drink, Jolene swiped her hands on her apron, wringing them to pull the moisture away.

"Good work today, Jo," Cat said. She slammed the cash register drawer with a bell-like *ding* and then swept her jet black hair into a handheld ponytail with one hand while fanning her face with the other. "Hotter than blue blazes in here with all the steam from that dang machine, yet you're still able to look remarkable. Tell me your secret, would ya? It's certainly not fair. In fact, I'm close to accusing you of some sort of magical sorcery. I've come to the conclusion that that's the only plausible explanation. Wizardry!"

Jolene didn't feel magical in any way other than the fact that she'd managed to not completely melt into a puddle. She considered that a big win. Years ago, she'd given up the fight between her hair and humidity and let the elements do their thing with her unruly tresses. Having a hairdresser who knew how to cut curly hair was also a game changer. It was totally wash and wear for Jolene and her chin-length, blonde ringlets that sprung out of her head in whichever direction they pleased.

"No secrets, Cat. Just dollar store shampoo and Merrylark's infamous hard water."

"Hard water, hmph," Cathy grumbled as she dropped her hair back down. She grabbed a wet rag and swept it over the counter, collecting crumbs and splattered coffee droplets left there from the busy morning. "Just one more thing *not* to love about these parts."

"Oh, but there are so, so many other reasons to love it here. I can easily put up with those stubborn water stains on shower doors and dinner plates if it means I get to live in the best place on earth." Jolene draped her hands onto Cat's rounded shoulders and gave a tiny squeeze before bringing her fingers back up to her own apron to untie it from her neck. She folded the fabric into square, even sections and handed it to Cat, her cue that she was informally clocking out. "Mind if I head out? I need to head home to get the lake house prepped for today's newest renter."

"You still taking care of that place? Gotta be a lot of work with tenants arriving every few days and all. Can't imagine it's much fun cleaning it up each week."

"I enjoy it, actually. Gives me something to do and new people to meet. It's my kind of gig."

"You never cease to amaze me, Jo. Always looking for that silver lining, even if you have to find it while scrubbing a toilet bowl."

Jolene flashed a bright, toothy smile. "Sometimes that's the only place it exists!"

2

LUKE

E VERY BUTTON LIT up the dashboard, like a retail store's Christmas window display on the fritz.

"Just a few more turns, Bessie. You can do it, girl. I promise I'll be good to you once we get there. Give you that oil you love so much and a nice, long bubble bath." The aging truck didn't appreciate the smooth talk and belched an indignant gurgle that shut her engine down like a plug pulled from the wall. The vehicle coasted to a stop on an icy tract of highway that was neither home nor destination for Luke Handley, but some unknown patch between. "Really? That's no way to treat the man who's taken such good care of you for the past ten years, Bessie. I really thought we had something here."

Luke dropped a palm to the dash, knowing it would do nothing, but often a man's first instinct was to swat an inanimate object if it wasn't working. That approach didn't work on Bessie. Luke was just about to start in with more nonsensical compliments as a Hail Mary when a truck just as beaten and worn as his sidled up next to him, its hazard lights blinking out a greeting of acknowledgment. While the trucks might've been the same in age, the span of half a century separated the drivers.

"Need a lift, son?" an elderly man asked as he hand-cranked the window down. His voice quivered but was still audible above the rumbly engine that burped and belched under the hood. Luke noticed a cross hanging from the rearview mirror, swinging like a pendulum set in motion. It flickered holograms of glittering light across the cab which filled his chest with the promise of hope. "Heading up to the lake?"

The thought of leaving Bessie alone on this foreign stretch of road didn't sit well in Luke's gut, but without the help of a tow truck to pull her the rest of the way, she wasn't going to budge, the frustrating mule that she was. Luke's options were few, the amount of people he'd passed on the road in the last hour even fewer.

He took this selfless offer from a stranger as a sign from the Big Man Upstairs that someone had his back.

"If the lake you're referring to is Merrylark and you've got room for one more traveler and a smelly old duffle bag, I'd be most grateful for the ride, sir."

"Hop in. This ol' sniffer doesn't work all too well these days, anyway, so you're in luck. Name's Roger Wilkins."

"Luke Handley."

"Like Cool Hand-*ley* Luke?" The man's wrinkled upper lip edged into a smile.

"Something like it."

Grabbing the brim of his ball cap between two fingers, Luke offered a sort of quick salute, and then strode to the back of the truck to toss his luggage into the rusted bed next to a toolbox and orange water jug. He returned to the front and yanked on the passenger door handle. The unoiled hinges moaned loudly, a squeal that drew his broad shoulders to his ears in instant reaction.

"What brings you to the lake, son?"

That question was a loaded one, and Luke wasn't up for offering the full explanation. "Just a much needed getaway."

"Well then, you've come to the right place. My 78 years in the same house, staring at the same glorious body of water might make me a little biased, but there's no better place to get away for the holidays than Merrylark. It's straight off a Christmas postcard."

Luke glanced across the cab and grinned at his new comrade, hoping the assertion was right. He rested his hands on the thighs of his faded blue jeans and swung his gaze out the frosted windshield. There was a crack clear across the middle, like it had been carved out of ice with the blade of an ice skate. Tall pines stretched skyward, flanking the twisting road on either side, hemming it in with thick green needles. Despite their sharp texture, they looked soft and calming as they blurred past the windows while they drove.

Luke hadn't come from the city, exactly, but the nature surrounding him here was different from the acres of dry pastureland that fanned out around his family's country farmhouse just three hours south in Kernlyville. While he loved their horses and their rescue facility, he'd gladly trade thundering hooves for the light prancing of deer and woodland creatures. Change of scenery—even if only temporary —was always a good thing.

Truth be told, Luke hadn't been exactly sure what to expect from Merrylark. The website nearly made it seem like something out of *Snow White and the Seven Dwarfs*, fairytale folklore at its best. It wouldn't have been his first choice, but he hadn't been the one to originally make the reservation. Even still, the trip had been booked—nonrefundable—and he'd be darned if he let it go to complete waste. From what he remembered from childhood, *Snow White* hadn't been all that bad. At least there was that happy, fairytale ending.

"Just another mile up ahead. What's the address where you're staying?"

Luke had to reach his hand into his shirt pocket to pull out the sheet of paper he'd remembered to grab off the printer at the last minute. "10 Spruce Way," he read.

"Ah! The O'Connell cottage. Of course. You'll love it." Roger's hands gripped the wheel tightly. "Jojo's been keeping it in great shape. Just got a new dock last summer. Brand new boards and posts and all that jazz. Best fishing in the lake is off that pier—left side, not right. Don't be surprised to wake up to find the locals casting their rods off it. It's quite the hotspot, even in these wintery temperatures."

"I didn't even think to bring a fishing pole," Luke admitted mostly to himself but out loud still. He was embarrassed by the statement since he would be spending a week at an actual lake with water and fish and boats and docks. Even six months after the fact, he hadn't been able to wrap his brain around the change in purpose for this trip. Originally, he hadn't figured he'd be spending any time outside of the cabin at all. Fishing had been far, far from his mind.

"Jojo will fix you up with some gear. No worries about that."

It took a moment for Luke's train of thought to shift back to the conversation at hand. He got stuck in the past more than he cared to admit. He snapped from his wayward thoughts. "Fishing gear. Sure. That would be nice. Appreciate it."

It turned out Bessie had almost proven her worth, stranding Luke just ten minutes away from his ultimate destination. Before he knew it, Roger's truck engine shut off in a slushy driveway belonging to a lake house that was a smaller version of the others surrounding it: a quaint, white-sided box with a tiny front stoop, outfitted with a brilliant, bright red door. It looked as though it could serve as the in-law quarters to the more expansive home just to its left.

"This is you." Roger nodded to the modest house. "Enjoy your stay, Luke. I'm just up the road at 18 Spruce if you need anything, but Jojo's pretty good at tending to her neighbors, so feel free to try her first. Plus, I know she appreciates the company. Especially this time of year."

Luke was grateful for the man who'd been a stranger up until fifteen minutes ago and he told him so. Though the time they'd spent together was limited, it was remarkable what a kind gesture could do for the soul, and Luke's soul had been in desperate need of this type of mending. Generosity wasn't dead and good people still existed. This was welcome news. He liked Merrylark already.

Just as the emailed instructions indicated, Luke found the key waiting for him under the rubber mat. Pine needles collected in the embossed word *Welcome*, so he lifted the mat to shake off the stray barbs. There was a metal screen door that he opened first, then he fumbled with the key and the lock while the weight of his duffel bag tugged downward on his shoulder. Jostling a bit, he shoved the strap higher. After teetering for a while, he finally settled his luggage onto the ground near his feet and used both hands to turn over the deadbolt.

"Work smarter, not harder, Handley," he half-scolded with a laugh as he shoved the key into the lock and swung the door wide.

The lake house smelled old, must trapped in the walls and furniture like it had been baked into the materials, marinating there for decades. Yet it wasn't at all unpleasant. In fact, Luke liked the smell. It smelled as a cottage should, worn with time and memories.

Even if the smell *had* been off-putting, the view more than made up for it. Along the west-facing wall of the home were floor-to-ceiling windows, expansive enough to outline the lake in its entirety like a gilded frame around a painting. Something about the scene—the icy blue water and the aluminum boats overturned on the docks—lowered Luke's blood pressure and loosened the tightness that had wound in his chest more fiercely than the curving roadway up here.

And even more inviting than the draw of the lake was the lone bottle of champagne perched on the butcher block counter. He wasn't really a bubbly-drinking kind of guy—couldn't recall ever actually having a glass of the stuff—but a drink was a drink and he needed one, desperately. After tossing his duffle bag on the plaid green and blue couch, he rummaged through the kitchen drawers to locate an opener. What he couldn't locate was an actual glass, but the bottle would be fine. He wouldn't be sharing.

Warmth slid through his veins with the first crisp sip. Relaxation came with the second. Several hearty chugs and he finally felt like he might be able to loosen up enough to enjoy himself on this trip. He'd have to come up with another name for it though, because honeymoon wasn't going to fly.

A *time out.*

That might best describe what he planned to do here. Or a sabbatical. Even better. His lifelong buddy, Craig McGraw, took one of those last semester. While the rest of Craig's coworkers had grumbled in the break room about the absent science teacher, Luke felt like Craig had been onto something with his scheduled removal from society.

A *sabbatical*. It didn't have a bad ring to it.

Luke was rolling around the new title for his vacation in his mind and on his tongue when he made the mistake of meandering down the only hallway toward the master bedroom. Immediately, he froze in the doorframe. The bed was huge—king-sized. One with notched and knotty logs for the posts and the frame, and the dresser and armoire matched in a similar style and feel. There was a bear motif, with a carved wooden cub placed on the nightstand for the base of a lamp and a stuffed teddy bear settled neatly on the center of the bed like some furry lake house mascot.

And sprinkled all around like confetti were crimson red rose petals. Hundreds of them. A bouquet full, probably, torn from their stems and scattered ceremoniously over the wedding bed.

Luke's face went hot.

Pivoting on the heel of his boot, he pulled the door shut, deciding the couch would be a perfectly fine place to sleep instead.

3

JOLENE

"**M**ARK?" JOLENE CALLED out as soon as she heard the unexpected knocking. There was a naïve hope in her voice, but it fell flat the moment she opened the door. The man standing before her—the one with the dirty white baseball cap, wary smile, and upturned palmful of crushed rose petals—didn't really even resemble her Mark. She wasn't sure why she'd said it. She just couldn't keep the name from falling from her lips each time she had a surprise visitor. It had become an inexplicable and instinctual habit of hers, to blurt out her hope without first protecting her heart.

"Nope. Not Mark. Luke, actually. But if we can find a Matthew and John we might have ourselves a pretty good start."

Jolene shook her head, tossing off the vision shrouding her reality. The man on her porch instantly snapped into view, like the grabbing adjustment and focus of a camera lens. He didn't look anything like Mark other than the light hair and lighter eyes, but even those were off. This man's eyes were blue, icy almost. And his skin was too tanned for this time of year, which hinted that its pigment was more genetic than sun given.

"Jolene, right?" His words weren't slurred, but they weren't distinct and separated as they should be. Rather, they bled together like they were strung along in a stanza of music, different notes in the same measure. She figured it was just his way of talking; lazily and relaxed. "You *are* Jolene, aren't you? I do have the right house? I'm not great with directions, but *next-door-neighbor* seemed easy enough to follow." He smiled again, this one more confident and sure, revealing brilliant white teeth behind full lips.

"Yes," Jolene stammered, aware she'd been practically gawking. She shook her head another time. "I'm sorry. Jolene. Jolene Carter."

Two hands jutted toward her. She glanced down to see the flower petals she'd used earlier that day as decorations now crumpled and offered back, like they were being returned at a department store counter.

"These," the man said as his hands crossed over the threshold and into her home, "I can't have these and they were too pretty to just throw away and my new friend Roger said you were helpful so I was hoping you might help me figure out what I can do with them that won't seem as wasteful as throwing them into the trash bin since they're so nice and all."

Those words—those were all spoken in one breath, like it was the last one he had and he had to get everything out before it ran out.

Jolene's mouth dropped open.

"I'm sorry," he said. He took all the petals and squished them into his left palm, freeing up his right so he could extend it in greeting. "Luke Handley. Your neighbor for the week. I'm staying in that house right next door." His head nudged toward the O'Connell place.

"Right," Jolene spoke. "Yes, Luke. I knew you were coming. I'm sorry to be so—"

"Surprised by the random man on your doorstep?"

"Have you been drinking?" Jolene quietly gasped at her own boldness the instant the words trickled out.

"Not nearly enough."

"I don't mean to insinuate that you have," Jolene stammered over his answer as she tried to regain some dignity. She felt that awful, sick tugging in her stomach from knowing she'd spoken with no filter. This man must've thought she was an utter fool, and a rude one at that. "That was just a really, really long sentence you spoke there."

All of the words Jolene offered felt like the wrong ones. She took his proffered hand into her grip and shook it, albeit hesitantly.

Luke only smiled. It was an honest, genial grin. "For what it's worth, I'm not drunk. Never really have been. You'd think an entire bottle would completely do me in, but this one seems to have no effect. Not that I didn't try."

"That bottle on the counter?" Jolene tried not to snicker as she began to comprehend what he was saying. "That was sparkling cider, Luke. I used to leave the real stuff for the guests, but that led to some pretty rowdy neighbors in the past."

Luke brought a hand to the back of his neck and rubbed at it in a way that made him look boyish and self-conscious. "Well that certainly explains it." He huffed out a laugh. "Probably for the best, anyway. I don't need to start off my sabbatical with a headache."

People came to Merrylark for all sorts of reasons, but sabbaticals usually weren't at the top of the list. Jolene hadn't recalled that information in Luke's reservation. In fact, if she remembered correctly, there was supposed to be one more tenant joining him during his weeklong stay.

"Sabbatical? As in from your job?"

"From my life."

"Wow," Jolene muttered before she could stop herself. And then she did the one thing she knew to do in a situation like this. "Luke, would you like to come in for a cup of coffee? I was just about to put a pot on."

Luke had been looking at the ground—at the *Welcome* mat that was a twin to the one on his stoop—but his gaze shot up with Jolene's remark. "Actually, even after all that cider, I really *could* use something to drink."

❄

JOLENE WASN'T USED to having male company other than Roger and she honestly didn't even consider him company anymore. Roger was family. In fact, most of the Merrylark residents were like family. It was a small, tight-knit community that stayed woven together even when tourists and vacationers periodically threaded their way into the tapestry during summer months and holidays. Jolene loved that. There was always room for a newcomer in these parts, and most of the time, they integrated so quickly it was like they were also long-time residents. There was just something so homey about Merrylark, for visitor and long-timer alike.

But Jolene rarely had these particular visitors in to share a cup of coffee. She was great at making sure the O'Connell place was a warm, inviting retreat. Often, those who rented the lake house never really needed to venture out for anything. It was all right there, provided and ready for their stay.

Maybe that's why she was so surprised to see Luke at her front door just a half an hour after his arrival.

In her kitchen, Jolene pulled the coffee grounds from the freezer, measured them out, and placed them into the maker, trying not to glance back at the handsome stranger standing in the center of her living room. Suddenly, she became insecure at the way Christmas had exploded within her house—how the eight-foot tree was not only flocked with fake, fluffy snow, but leaning like the Tower of Pisa from the uneven weight of hundreds of handmade ornaments and kitschy decorations. Every flat surface in her home boasted a snowman figurine or Santa sculpture. The sofa table was adorned with a ceramic sleigh, with eight reindeer to pull the load and there was the customary antique train that circled the skirt of the tree, chugging 'round and 'round on the plastic tracks. It even blew a faint little whistle every few minutes, creating a holiday soundtrack of tidings and cheer.

Christmas was Jolene's favorite time of year and her home was a visual testament to that.

"A lot of those decorations were handed down," she said, feeling the need to offer an excuse for why her place rivaled the splendor of the North Pole. "Some were gifts. Others I got after Christmas for like fifty percent off or at thrift stores or garage sales."

"I think it's perfect," Luke commented as he touched one of the glittering ball ornaments on the tree with the tip of his index finger. He looked over his shoulder at Jolene and she felt a low flutter in her stomach when their gazes connected. She rapidly broke from his stare.

"Makes me almost wish my place had a tree," Luke confessed with a nonchalant shrug.

"A tree!" Jolene exclaimed. "We can totally get you a tree! I'm so sorry I didn't even think to do that. Of course you'd want a tree. I was so focused on restocking the toilet paper that a Christmas tree totally slipped my mind!"

"I wasn't complaining, Jolene." Hearing her name spoken in his deep, yet intimately soft, drawl made Jolene suddenly hot. It could've been the steam from the brewing coffee, but she doubted it. "And thank you for the T.P. That's a much appreciated necessity," he said, winking in a way that looked so effortless and natural on him. "A tree would be nice, though. You happen to know where I can find one?"

"Of course I do!" Tree shopping was at the very top of Jolene's list of favorite Christmas traditions. "There's a little lot down on Glenn Street that I can take you to tomorrow. Not a huge variety, but they'll have what you need."

"That would be great. S'pose I'll need to grab a few ornaments when we're in town too. Forgot to pack those in my suitcase." Luke chuckled.

"Goodness, I think I could just give you a few of mine." Jolene hovered over the coffee pot, unsure where to place her body within her own home and she laughed in a way that felt forced and phony. She'd never felt so awkward within these walls before and knew this man was the reason for her blunder. He rattled something deep in her nerves.

"I'm not going to take your ornaments."

"Oh, I have more than a few to spare," she admitted. "Plus, it'll be good to thin it out a little. I always feel bad for ones in the back that never get any attention."

Luke slowly turned to face her. "You feel bad for the ornaments?"

"Hey, you're the guy who came over with a handful of

rose petals you couldn't bring yourself to throw away. I'd say we're even."

"True. True." Luke still had the flowers in his palm, and at that moment he placed them onto an empty candy dish that looked like a ceramic peppermint in a twisted cellophane wrapper. He glanced down at the discarded petals and then up to Jolene. "That coffee almost ready?"

Just then, the machine beeped as the last of the carafe filled up. "Speak of the devil." Jolene clapped her hands together in small celebration and then opened the cupboard to retrieve two mugs from the top shelf. "How do you take it?"

"Black."

Jolene wished she could read a man by the way he drank his coffee because she wanted to know more about this particular one in front of her. She rarely fraternized with the O'Connell tenants, but she couldn't say she was upset to have this surprise visitor. He seemed polite enough—courteous, even—and although Jolene was content to be alone most of the time, during the holidays that aloneness inevitably turned into loneliness. It was just the way of things.

She brought Luke his coffee and gestured toward the corduroy couch where they both lowered to sit. It felt a little too formal, so Jolene kicked off her ballet flats and tucked her legs up underneath her body to cozy into the cushions and pillows there. Steam rose from her mug and she cooled it with a breath blown between her pursed lips. Wrapping her fingers around the warm ceramic, she looked over at her new neighbor. He was cooling his drink the same way.

"I'm really sorry to come over here like this." Luke's light eyes creased at the corners, his strong brow furrowing noticeably in thought. "To intrude on your evening and all."

"Right, because I have *so* much going on," Jolene said in a voice thick with so much sarcasm she feared she sounded pathetic. "I mean, I do stuff occasionally. I'm not like a shut-in or anything."

Luke laughed. "Didn't figure you were." He leaned forward to rest his coffee mug on a square tile coaster on the table in front of them. "Tomorrow then? You'll take me on a hunt for the perfect tree?"

"Absolutely, although I can't promise perfection. Merrylark is known for a lot, but our Christmas tree offerings leave much to be desired. You'll be able to take your pick, but you won't have a lot to pick from."

"I'm sure whatever we find will be just fine," Luke said through a smile that made Jolene's cheeks flush. "If it's even one-tenth as nice as yours, it'll be the finest Christmas tree I've ever owned."

For a girl who loved Christmas more than any other day of the year, that was the best compliment Jolene could ever receive.

"THAT'LL BE three-hundred fifty."

"Dollars?" Luke's jaw came unhinged.

"Yesiree." The tow truck driver didn't look up from the metal clipboard in his thick hands. He had grease in the creases of his knuckles, like he'd dipped his hands in black ink. The driver continued scratching a pen across the paper clipped to the surface and it reminded Luke of the time he was pulled over last year and the cop wrote up his traffic ticket, never making eye contact as he jotted down his fine.

"As in three-hundred and fifty U.S. dollars?" Luke asked again, just to verify.

"Yes." The man's posture didn't change but his eyes angled up and met Luke's in an intense, intimidating stare that caused Luke's Adam's apple to bob with a tight swallow. "*U.S. dollars.*"

Luke wasn't a cheap guy, but he wasn't loaded either, and the type of money the hauler demanded wasn't something he readily had on hand to blow. He'd have to work a few more odd jobs once he returned home to make up for the unexpected cost of pulling Bessie up the mountain.

"You take credit card?"

"Sir, I'll take just about anything short of your firstborn if it'll get you stop with the questions. I've got two other vehicles stranded on the mountainside and I'm the only tow truck in town. In a hundred-mile radius, to be exact. Time is money and you're currently wasting mine."

Luke took the hint and pulled his wallet from his back pocket. Two of the cards in his billfold had expired last month and the third was creeping perilously close to its limit. He didn't have any other options. Luke flicked the plastic card toward the driver and felt his lungs squeeze with a suspended breath while he watched the man swipe it through the card reader plugged into his cell phone.

"Just need your signature here."

The driver flashed the face of the device Luke's way. A sigh of relief slipped through Luke's lips, thankful that particular card hadn't been declined. "Thanks again for bringing her up the hill. I'm not sure what the issue is but I bet I can get her running again in—"

"Aren't we all done here?" The man was already backing away. If it had been a phone conversation rather than a face-to-face interaction, Luke would've been hung up on by now. "I really gotta get going."

"Yes. Right. I appreciate the haul. Hopefully I won't need another one."

"Hopefully not," the driver said with the widest, rolling eyes Luke had ever witnessed on a grown man. He thought he should congratulate him on successfully keeping his eyeballs in his head after that exaggerated gesture. It was downright impressive.

In any other scenario, Luke would've been offended. He considered himself to be a nice guy and people generally liked him. He wasn't the sort to experience road rage. He returned books to the library on time, sometimes even early. He held doors open and put the toilet seat down and threw away expired milk rather than leave it in the refrigerator after its date had passed. He was courteous. Some would label him kind.

But there were always people in life who just didn't like you, no matter how decent you were.

His ex-fiancé was one of those.

It hadn't always been that way between them. After all, Kiara had gladly accepted the flawless carat on her left ring finger this time last year. There was no hesitation in the "yes" she shouted the moment he'd dropped down onto one knee, his proposal speech not yet even underway.

But somewhere along the line she *stopped* liking him. Stopped loving him. Or rather, she didn't like him quite as much as she liked her job as a CPA and the opportunities she saw for herself there. Unfortunately, when it came to love, second place was still the loser's position.

Luke promised himself he wouldn't allow this honeymoon week to hold his joy captive, though. Sure, it wasn't the trip he'd originally had in mind, but he wasn't going to let the painful memories turn this into a week full of painful "what ifs." He'd made a deliberate choice to keep that from happening.

Maybe that's why he'd been so quick to ask Jolene for a little help. The moment he set foot into her lovely home, he felt the one thing that had been sucked out of his life when Kiara called it quits on their future.

Joy.

Jolene's place was overflowing with it. Some might have been manufactured, what with the nostalgia that inherently went along with Christmas décor, but Luke felt it still, and that was more than he'd felt in a long, long while.

Jolene seemed like a nice woman, too. From their limited interaction, she didn't come across as a person who kept much to herself. She seemed sincere and vulnerable in a way that Luke hadn't expected from a perfect stranger. Kiara had never been that way. She'd always selected her words carefully, no differently from the way she'd selected their China pattern and bed sheet thread count for their wedding registry. Everything was planned out methodically and with purpose.

In the beginning, Luke liked that about Kiara the most. She was stable and consistent. Until she wasn't. Until she'd done the most inconsistent thing imaginable. Until she'd told him she was taking a promotion in New York City and she called off their winter wedding.

Luke threw open the hood to his truck and hit his hand against the vehicle. It would've been one thing if Kiara had chosen someone else. That, he might've been able to handle. But to lose to a career and the lure of the big city made what they had feel so insignificant and small. It would take a discipline Luke didn't know if he could muster to keep these sad thoughts from his mind this week. Distraction would be the key. What better way to distract himself than with a little holiday cheer?

❄

THE SUN HAD already set by the time Luke walked over to Jolene's place. Along with the dropping sun, the temperature followed suit and brought a bite to the air that reddened Luke's cheeks and made his nose tingle as though he was about to sneeze. He brought his hands to his mouth and cupped them there to let out a hot breath at the same moment Jolene opened her front door.

The smile she wore made his cheeks feel as red as they likely looked.

"Luke!" Even though he was certain they'd planned on this particular time to meet, she still appeared surprised to see him standing on her stoop. Or maybe it was excitement he detected in her voice. Luke had a hard time deciphering, but the hug she threw around his neck led him to believe it was a little of both. "I am *so* ready for this! I've been thinking about it all day! Can't wait!"

He couldn't get over how cute Jolene was, how she clasped her hands together by her chest like she was about to burst. It was the first time he'd thought this about another woman and not felt guilty for it. He hadn't noticed anyone other than Kiara for so long. Even after the split, his heart wasn't able to let go of the dreams they'd made together. But slowly, plan by plan, he'd pulled down every expectation like they were pieces of brick in a house built of their future. It was completely demolished now, but the hopes of a rebuild didn't feel so farfetched when he thought about spending time with a woman like Jolene.

Luke snapped from his thoughts and shook his head.

"Oh." Jolene took a step back, misreading his gesture. "We're not going anymore?"

"No, no. We're definitely going. Sorry. Mind wandered a bit there."

Her face, which had temporary drained of all emotion, regained its merry composure. "Oh, good! Not that it's like I didn't have anything else to think about today, but this definitely occupied most of my thoughts. There's nothing better than picking out a tree! Randy said they got in a brand new shipment from Oregon just this afternoon, so you'll have lots to choose from. It'll be great!"

"In that case, I'm glad I'll have someone to help in the

decision making process," Luke admitted. Conversation was so effortless between the two that it felt like they'd known each other much longer than twenty-four short hours. "Shoot," he said, suddenly realizing his predicament. "I completely forgot—Bessie's shot. I don't actually have a vehicle to put a tree in. How will this work?"

"Bessie?" Jolene's head cocked in a tilt. "Your car has a name? Why am I not surprised by that?"

"What? Does that reveal some sort of deep, hidden mystery about me?"

"Not necessarily. It's just all the guys I've known who name their cars tend to be a little compulsive about their vehicles. Like they'd do anything for them."

"As in drop $350 just to have her towed ten miles?"

Jolene's mouth thinned into a line. "Oh no. Please tell me you didn't let Hank swindle you out of that much money."

"If by Hank you're referring to a middle-aged, gruff ogre of a man, I'm afraid I've been swindled."

"Ogre!" Jolene shrieked a laugh and then socked Luke in the shoulder which took him by so much surprise he had to widen his stance and plant his feet to keep from falling over. For a little thing, Jolene packed an impressive punch. "Hilarious! Ogre is such an accurate description. Don't worry, I'll talk to my cousin and see if I can get some of that back for you. He's not as cantankerous as he looks."

"Your cousin?" Luke gaped. "Please don't tell me I just called your cousin an ogre."

"No, no, he's definitely ogre-ish. Plus, I just called him cantankerous, which isn't any nicer," Jolene said. "And I use the term cousin loosely. We're like fourth-cousins twice removed or something along those lines. Years ago his wife, Tilly, did a bunch of genealogy work and I somehow showed up as a twig on a branch of their tree. It's more of a joke than an actual relationship status, but Hank is devout when it comes to his family, so if I need a favor, I'll get it. That's the way it works with him."

"I'd hate for you to waste a favor for me."

"It's no waste at all."

Luke tried not to read into her comment, but it made him smile all the same.

"And about the truck," Jolene continued on beat, "we won't need one. Randy can deliver your tree. They have lots of guys that help work the lot. We're good to go."

"This town really is out of a fairytale."

"Hardly, but we do look out for one another and maybe that's something that only exists in fairytales anymore." Jolene side-stepped around Luke and skipped down the path toward her car parked in the gravel driveway: a green hatchback with California plates. She clicked her key fob to unlock the doors. At the sound of the beep, a massive dog came barreling around the back corner of Jolene's house and jumped into the last row of the vehicle just as Jolene opened the door to allow him in. "This is Ace," she said, shutting the door behind the animal. "So tell me a little about where you come from? Small town or big?"

"Not really a town at all." Luke took his place in the passenger's seat and pulled the belt across his body. He could feel the hot breath of the mutt on his ear and shrugged up his shoulders to block it.

"Ace!" Jolene shoved at the furry animal, ordering him to the back of the car with her elbow. "Leave Luke alone. He doesn't need your slobber all over that nice coat of his," she said as she smiled Luke's direction. "Go ahead. Tell me what home is to you."

"Well, my family runs a mustang rescue on about a

hundred and fifty acres down in the valley. We have to drive pretty far to get to the city and that's where we do the bulk of our shopping and things like that. There's a little strip along the highway that I suppose could have a small town feel to it, but it's nothing like this place. No real charm to be heard of, just a gas station and convenience store. Feed store. Stuff like that."

"So you *are* a cowboy. I thought I was getting that vibe from you."

"S'pose so, but mostly by osmosis. Our ranch goes back to my great-great grandpa. It's all I've ever really known, so it's sorta what I've become."

Just like the night before, Luke found himself sliding easily into laid back conversation with Jolene and he hardly noticed the time passing as they drove the forest hemmed roads toward town and Glenn Street. Ace kept mostly to himself in the back, but his breathing was warm and loud and fogged up the windshield like a sauna that made it difficult to see out. To Luke, Ace seemed like a happy-go-lucky kind of dog which felt like the perfect match for Jolene. He wouldn't have expected anything different from her pet.

"So, what brought a cowboy like you to a place like Merrylark?" Jolene asked after a few moments of quiet that Luke had filled by silently admiring the scenery as it rushed past. That postcard description Roger had used wasn't an exaggeration at all. This place boasted of a beauty that was such a juxtaposition to the dirt landscape Luke was accustomed to seeing day in and day out from the seat of a saddle.

"What brought me here? A girl."

Jolene's face paled. She looked like she was about to ask for clarification, but that didn't come and instead she kept quiet while she pulled into an open parking spot along a quaint shop-lined street. Glenn Street, Luke gathered.

Lampposts were wrapped in leafy garland, storefronts were painted with cheerful holiday scenes, and Salvation Army bells chimed in the distance as the soundtrack of the season. It was already Christmas in Merrylark, and it was stunning.

"We're here." Jolene unclicked her seatbelt. "Just a block up on the corner."

Luke was grateful she let his cryptic comment be. He wasn't ready to talk. Maybe Jolene sensed that, or maybe she was offering him the privacy she would have desired if the tables of conversation had been turned. Whatever the reason, Luke liked her all the more for it, and he'd already found himself liking her more than he dared to admit.

5

JOLENE

RANDY PIPER'S TREE selection was right on the money. Within five minutes, Luke chose a nice Douglas Fir just a foot taller than his six-foot-two frame. He graciously declined the free flocking that Randy threw in as a welcoming gesture to the town's newest occupant, stating that he didn't want to make a mess of the rental house.

After the tree had been picked and scheduled for delivery to the lake house the following morning, Jolene, Luke and Ace explored the small downtown, walking up the street one way and down it on the other side. There wasn't much to show off, but Jolene took pride in each store she knew the exact history and owners of. If Luke hadn't cared to hear the details, he didn't let it be known. He would smile in all the right places, laugh where appropriate, and exchange pleasantries with the many people Jolene was certain he'd forget the names of by the next day.

Even though she loved it here, over the years, the thought of leaving Merrylark had been a very real one for Jolene. She would mull it over each summer when the housing market was at its fullest, when she could get the most money for her place had she decided to sell. She'd map out a life that didn't involve the lake or the memories she couldn't escape while still residing within its zip code. But a life anywhere else, even removed from the daily remembrance of past pain, felt unexpectedly more painful. Unbearable. Unrealistic.

Life involved pain, that was the nitty-gritty truth of it. And sometimes being surrounded by those who knew the details of your pain—who witnessed and lived it out right alongside you—eased it, if only a little. Starting over in a new place where she'd have to explain herself and her situation wasn't at all appealing. Though she'd gotten good at the one paragraph summary of her life, it wasn't one she favored retelling.

"So," Luke said as they neared the end of the block. Jolene's parked car was just on the other side. Several shops had closed down for the night, their lights blinking out and OPEN signs now flipped to read CLOSED. "Want to grab coffee or a drink before we head back?"

"Would you believe the one thing we don't have here is a proper coffee shop? My friend, Cat, has her truck, but most days she's traveling out of town or working other venues with it. There's Sal's Diner and you can get a cup of coffee there, but that's not their specialty and the atmosphere isn't exactly what I'd call a relaxing one. We've got a little bit of everything, but a coffee house isn't on the list."

"No coffee shop?" Luke looked almost offended. "How is that even possible?"

Jolene shrugged. Her hands were deep in her coat pockets and she buried her chin in the red wool scarf tugged around her neck. It was cold—getting colder by the minute —and the idea of curling up with a warm drink and good conversation felt like just the right prescription for a frigid night like this one. "Gosh, I honestly don't know. In some ways I think we're lucky we haven't succumbed to the whole commercialized shop on every corner bit, but I agree, it would be nice to have a quaint little place to get a decent cup and hang out for a bit. The town could use that, no question. I could use that."

"So why haven't you opened it yet?" Luke playfully jabbed his elbow into her side.

"Me? Oh goodness, no. I can brew a pot of coffee and hand out orders for Cat when she needs me, but I certainly can't craft a cappuccino or draw those fancy foam designs or anything." She laughed again and shook her head as though confirming her own self-assessment. "No, no I'm definitely not the best candidate to open that up. I've always dreamt of a place like that for Merrylark, one where everyone can gather together, but I'm certainly not the right woman for the job."

Luke let it go and just smiled quietly to himself, which caused Jolene to do the same. Minutes passed and their pace slowed, both seeming to know the longer they drew out their steps, the longer they'd have together. Ace was the only one who was in any sort of hurry, but he was a dog of routine and it was well past his dinnertime. His growling stomach guided his legs and the pull on the leash tugged Jolene forward, making her arm outstretch more than was comfortable. She wasn't going to let her dog rush her evening. She gave one swift jerk on the leash and halted Ace's quick moves.

"I guess we should head back?" Luke spoke it as a question, but Jolene didn't have an answer for it. She wanted to prolong their evening, but there just wasn't much left to do in town. She'd accompanied him to select his tree and that was the end of her obligation. Nothing about spending time with Luke felt like an obligation, though. It felt fantastic and comfortable and restful, like she could finally catch her breath and let it slowly back out.

But then the gasp she let out instead wiped all of that away.

"Oh no!" she shouted, planting her feet on the pavement underneath her like she'd screeched her car brakes. "Mildred!"

"Mildred?" Luke's eyebrows drew together.

"Shoot! What time is it?"

"Seven-fifteen."

Jolene's mouth squiggled into a frown, her chin tense and worried. "We have to go. I was supposed to be at Mildred's at seven. I'll get you home and then head back out. I'm so sorry. This is terrible of me. I'm usually not so forgetful. Our evening just got away from me."

Looking at her with soft, thoughtful yet still bewildered eyes, Luke said, "Or you could just take me with you."

"To Mildred's?" Jolene's chin pulled back into her scarf, swallowed in the billowing fabric. "You don't want to go to Mildred's, Luke. I promise you won't have any fun. It'll be boring and sloggy and dull. Mostly boring."

"Sloggy?"

"Like the time will just slog along."

Leaning toward her so his face was just inches away, Luke said, "Well, now I have to go just to find out exactly what you mean when you say *slog*."

"I'm pretty sure I didn't use that in the right context. I'm just trying to dissuade you from being stuck in an evening you can't get out of."

Reaching out, Luke squeezed the hand that held securely to Ace's leash. Jolene startled while he grinned and said, "If I get to spend more time with you, I'll happily slog along."

✳

"I JUST CAN'T decide if this is my color." Luke rolled the small bottle between his thumb and index finger and slanted his eyes like he was studying the polish, really weighing his options.

Jolene glanced up from her work and tried not to laugh. She'd already bumped Mildred's hand once earlier and had to start over completely. Patience was not one of Mildred's few virtues, and there was no way the woman would last through another drying. Her red sparkly polish was just barely tacky and only needed a few more minutes before Jolene felt confident Mildred could go about her business without smudging her freshly manicured nails. She'd already promised Mildred a small piece of chocolate if she remained still. She'd have to dole out an entire candy bar if the nail painting required a redo.

"I think silver for you." Mildred had the voice of someone who's speech had been damaged with years of smoke and addiction. It was raw and gravely and hinted at a past Jolene could only venture a guess about. Like many of Merrylark's residents, Mildred came to the lake to escape a life somewhere else. She'd found out—as everyone who moved to town did—that the picture-perfect reputation wasn't a fabrication. It was the real deal. She never left town after that discovery, and that had been fifty-two years prior.

Jolene's gut panged with the realization that she'd toyed with the idea of escaping the very place most people seemed to escape *to*. Where was the sense in that?

"Silver? Yeah? You think so?" Luke rummaged through

the plastic tub of half-used polish bottles. "Not magenta or teal? How about this one? Doubly Bubbly Bubble Gum."

"Silver," Mildred ordered. "Matches all those flecks in your hair."

"Luke does not have silver hair, Millie," Jolene hissed, her tone hushed and under a breath. She'd grown to love her old friend and even her acerbic tongue, but she didn't want to offend Luke. He'd been nothing but a gentleman tonight and she knew Mildred had the distinct ability to turn their evening from sweet to sour in an instant.

"No, no, Mildred's right, Jolene. I do have a stray gray hair or two."

"Or thirty-two," Mildred croaked. She blew across her nail beds while fanning out her crooked fingers, waggling them back and forth to speed up the process.

"Or apparently thirty-two, which is fitting since that's how old I am. One for every year."

Jolene had wondered Luke's age but felt awkward asking it. She was grateful for the roundabout way of gathering that information, even if it had been in the form of Mildred's insults. Luke was just three years older than she and that felt appropriate, though she wasn't sure why she was thinking in terms of what was and wasn't appropriate between them. Surely *that* wasn't appropriate.

"I wouldn't call it silver. More like flecks of salt and pepper," Jolene finally offered. She smiled up at Luke from across the sticky kitchen table that had become their makeshift nail salon. When their eyes met, she didn't pull away like she'd done the night before. She allowed herself to really look at him, and he was even more handsome than she'd noticed at first. His jaw was square, defined and sharp. A dusting of stubble covered it in just the right way that was ruggedly masculine but still looked like it could be soft under her fingertips. He had full lips that remained plump even when pulled into a smile, and his light eyes disappeared each time he grinned, scrunching at the corners to make him seem friendly and approachable. He was nice to look at and easy to admire and Jolene found herself doing a bit of both.

But then Mildred belched—a wet, opened mouthed burp. Ace startled and barked from his cozy place on the floor next to them and Jolene blinked away from her stare that had embarrassingly turned into gawking.

"Salt and pepper?" Mildred snapped, burping again and then hitting her chest with her fist like she had indigestion. "For heaven's sake, Jolene, his head isn't a spice drawer. He doesn't have seasonings; he's got gray hair!"

Jolene wondered if Mildred had ever been a nice woman or if age slowly took that from her, too, like it had when it robbed her of her strength, her faculties, her memory. Maybe manners were just additional things to lose as the years dwindled down. But Jolene knew many elderly people who were kind and generous, despite life sometimes being harder and harsher on them. Roger was the prime example. That knowledge only made her more determined to show kindness and generosity to those who naturally lacked it, no matter their age, no matter their behavior.

Mildred needed Jolene's friendship, so she would give it to her. She'd been doing just that for nearly ten years now.

"Are we just about done here?" The old woman moved to touch one of her nails. Jolene stopped her immediately. The last thing she wanted to do was sit and wait while another set of touch-ups dried. With light strokes, Jolene swept the pad of her thumb over Mildred's index fingernail and was relieved when it came back clean.

"Yep. All done." She squeezed and then released

Mildred's hand. "Anything else we can do for you before we get going?"

"Cat litter needs changing—"

"Show me the way." Luke pushed back from the table and stood. Apparently manual labor was more his thing than pampering. "Just point me in the right direction and I'll get it taken care of."

Jolene sprang from her chair and scurried over to Luke, gently taking him by the elbow and out of Mildred's earshot. "You don't have to do that, Luke. Seriously. Head out to the car and I'll meet you and Ace in five minutes. You must be dying of boredom already after our evening at the salon." She made air quotes around her last words. "Let me do it. I won't be long."

"It's no big deal, Jolene. Honestly. I scoop horse poop daily back at the ranch. Emptying a litter box isn't going to kill me."

"She has fourteen cats."

"Okay, well, I'll plug my nose."

Jolene's hand was still on Luke's arm and she squeezed it in a 'thank-you' sort of way. "I'll get things cleaned up here and then I can get you back to the lake house. It's later than I realized. I'm sorry the night has been so much longer than we originally planned."

"I'm not," Luke said and then he'd disappeared into the laundry room where Mildred had told him the cat box was located.

While Jolene put the paper towel roll back in its place in the kitchen next to Mildred's sink which overflowed with crusty dishes, she tried not to let her heart beat at the rate it threatened to beat. It wanted to race right out of her chest. She wouldn't allow it. Sure, Luke was handsome. He was more polite than other past O'Connell tenants and he paid more attention to her than any man had in a long time. But he had a one-week reservation. That was it. He'd head home. Jolene sincerely doubted he wanted to spend his time —time he was paying for—with a quirky woman in her late twenties and her eclectic bunch of friends, dog included.

She'd make sure not to bother him tomorrow. He deserved his space and she'd encroached on that. Tomorrow Jolene would keep to herself and let Luke enjoy the sabbatical he had planned. While tonight had been fun, memorable even, tomorrow things would go back to normal and that would be okay.

At least she could pretend it would be.

6

LUKE

L UKE PRAYED TO the truck gods that it was just the ignition switch. He could afford that. Unfortunately, all signs pointed to the transmission, a much larger bill and longer time in the shop. It wasn't looking good for Bessie. He'd gotten up early to start the diagnostic process. His breakfast was a stale apple cinnamon cereal bar he'd thrown into his duffel bag and a glass of water from the tap. He liked the way the water tasted. It was crisper, cleaner, and lacked the metallic bite of the water he was used to back home. Of course even the water would be better here. He half-expected to see a magnet on the cottage refrigerator that read, *"Everything's Better in Merrylark."* That was the impression he was quickly forming. Merrylark seemed near perfect, other than Hank's abruptness and Mildred's harmless teasing. Every town had a few sour apples.

Luke figured the breakfast bar wouldn't tide him over long, and after a few hours, he felt the hollow growl scratching at his stomach in confirmation. He wondered what he would do for lunch without a full fridge or any way to get to the store to stock it. His thoughts immediately went to Jolene. She probably had plans already. He couldn't assume she'd be free or even interested in spending more time with him. Maybe he'd venture a few doors down to see if Roger wanted to grab a bite once things were figured out with the truck. That sounded like a decent enough plan.

Just then, the rumble of a motor pulled his attention from the engine in front of him. He pushed off the vehicle and wiped his greasy hands with a nearby rag. A large green truck with a Christmas tree sticking out of the bed drove up behind his and stopped just a few feet away.

"Hey brother, mind giving me a hand?" A young man, probably in his mid-twenties, hollered as he hopped down from the cab. He slipped two leather gloves onto his hands and tossed Luke another pair, which Luke caught against his chest like a football. "I'm guessing it's going in the house?"

Luke laughed. "Probably the best place for it."

"Devon Manning." The man shoved a hand forward. "Luke Handley, I gather? The proud new owner of this seven-and-a-half foot Douglas Fir, fresh from the Oregon countryside?"

"That would be me."

"Good, good. Let's get this thing set up for you. She's a beaut."

The two men untied and pulled the tree down from the back of the truck, Luke in the front leading the way as he held the tapered end of the evergreen. Devon hoisted the thick trunk over his right shoulder. Shards of bark stuck to his black and red checkered flannel and a few pine needles caught in the impressive dark beard that fit Devon's overall look so well. To Luke, he was the epitome of a lumberjack, which reminded him that to Jolene, Luke was the quintessential cowboy. Best not to label someone so quickly, he thought. There was always more than initially met the eye.

Once inside, Luke realized there was really only one spot for the tree and that was the living room. He liked the way the windows would frame it in and wondered if, once decorated, a boater on the other side of lake would be able to see the twinkling lights from the opposite shores. He was excited to have a bit of Christmas in the lake house and the tree was the first step.

"These things suck up loads of water, so be sure to keep her hydrated and she'll last you well into the new year."

Luke slipped the gloves off his hands and gave them back. "Well, she'll only need to last me a week because that's all I'm here for. If I can get Bessie up and running again, that is."

"The truck parked in the driveway?"

"That'd be her."

"Mind if I take a look?" Devon brushed at his shirt, picking off the rogue pine needles from the fabric. Luke watched them spiral to the floor but wasn't at all bothered by the mess it created. It would give him an excuse to visit Jolene to borrow a vacuum. During his cursory tour of the house yesterday, that was one item he hadn't located.

"Be my guest. I think I've got it narrowed down to the ignition switch or transmission."

"What about the alternator?"

"You know? You might be onto something with that. Sure hope so, at least. That would be a heck of a lot less expensive than the transmission. I'd already started researching how to properly donate a kidney in order to pay for it."

Devon laughed at the remark. "There are lots of other things it could be besides the transmission. Let me have a look at her before you start selling off your organs. If you don't mind."

"Not at all." Luke followed Devon out the front door and down the path. The air was cold again, with a wind that wasn't blustery, but wasn't breezy either. Somewhere right in between that felt appropriate for the time of year. "I wish I could offer you something to drink while you work, but I haven't been able to get to the store just yet."

"What with the dead truck and all?"

"Ouch." Luke clutched at his chest in jest. "Bessie? Dead? Really?"

"Sorry, brother. I mean, with your girl under the weather."

Luke appreciated Devon's humor and slapped a friendly palm to his back. "That I can deal with. I've promised her in sickness and in health but I'm not ready for the whole until death do us part thing."

"How 'bout this?" Devon pulled his gloves from his back jeans pocket and put them on again. He peered under the open hood and leaned forward to gain a better view. "If I can figure out what's wrong with your girl, you buy me lunch. If you figure it out, I'll buy lunch. Deal?"

Luke liked that idea. His stomach liked it even better. "Deal."

※

"FUEL PUMP. NEVER would've suspected that," Devon muttered between mouthfuls of a French dip he tore into like he was worried Luke was going to take it from him. He picked up a fry and plunged it into a saucer of ketchup and then raised it to his beard-framed mouth as he said, "Congratulations, brother. Nice work figuring that one out. Mechanic status, right there."

Luke tipped his drink toward Devon. "Thanks. I should've thought of it in the beginning. Not sure why I didn't. I guess I'm more used to trouble-shooting lame horses these days than I am fixing rundown vehicles."

"That what you do back home? Got some land or something?"

Bringing his glass to his lips, Luke took a swallow. "My family does. I do a little bit of everything there. Guess the formal term would be a ranch hand, but that doesn't really do a lot to explain it now, does it?"

"Nah, I get it. I'm the small-town equivalent of that. Not quite a handy man. More of a go-to guy. Deliver trees during the Christmas season. Fix planters in the springtime. Repair docks and boat propellers and things like that. I've never had the need for a business card or ad in the paper. Somehow everyone just knows to call on me when they need something. That's the way it's always been."

Luke set his glass down and stretched his arms out onto the table. Sal's Diner was busy in a lunch-time-rush sort of way and it had been a while since their waitress tended to them. He'd wanted to order dessert, but hadn't been able to flag her down yet.

"You've lived in Merrylark your whole life?" Luke asked, wondering if he was prying. Devon didn't seem to think so.

"Born and raised."

"That the case for most people here?" Now he was definitely prying, but the information he hoped to gain wasn't about Devon.

"I'd say fifty-fifty. Lots are second or third generation Merrylarkers, while others visited once and never left." Devon swiped at his mouth with a napkin and then crumpled it in his hand. "What brings you here? Not often a single guy rents the O'Connell cottage. Not since Mark, really, and that was over five years ago."

Luke bristled at the name, knowing he'd heard it before.

"Some sort of vacation?" Devon continued, not noticing Luke's fleeting reaction. "Mountain getaway?"

"Sabbatical." Luke lifted his finger into the air to draw the attention of the waitress that rushed past, carrying a tray full of food for other customers. She didn't even make eye contact.

"Cowboy sabbatical? Now that doesn't sound right. Not at all. We gotta come up with a different name for that." Devon thumbed at his wiry beard. "How about 'ranch hand respite'? Got a better ring to it, right?"

It did sound better, but it was a lie all the same.

"Ranch hand respite. I like it."

"So what exactly does a respite involve? Lots of reading? Staring at the lake? Yoga?" Devon took a drink of his beer which was almost gone. "Gotta be honest with you, brother, I'm not one to relax so I'm not even sure how it's supposed to go. Do you have to meditate or something like that? Do deep breathing exercises and wear lots of spandex?"

Luke and Devon were obviously cut from the same cloth. Luke didn't know how to let his mind and body rest either, never had. There really wasn't any time for it back home with duties starting at sunup and lasting well after sundown, when the night air was deep and bitter and cut through him, carving at his lungs and prickling his fingertips with frostbite. Even when chores and farm work were done, his muscles didn't slowly ease out of their fatigued state. They shut off completely when he collapsed into bed. That wasn't considered rest, that was necessity. Luke had two switches—ON and OFF, without any pause button between.

When he'd been engaged to Kiara, she kept him busy in any small amount of downtime that he would've had. There was always a schedule and she made sure he adhered to it. They even shared online calendars, where the day's events would pop up on their smartphones in varying colors, all coded for specific activities. Meals were yellow. Errands were red. Activities were blue. Quality time was green. Work was orange.

When she'd gone ahead and planned their honeymoon, Luke figured it would just look like a similar version of their days at home. He was along for the ride, which didn't bother him until the day she'd decided to put the brakes on it all.

"Truth be told, I don't really know how to relax either. Let's just say, I'm not glad Bessie broke down, but it'll give me something to fill the hours, at least."

The frazzled waitress rushed by again and Luke shot out a hand to call her over, but like before, he went unnoticed. It looked like he wasn't going to get that dessert he craved.

Devon threw back the last swallow of his drink and settled the empty glass onto the table. "You know, if you're looking for something to keep you busy, there's a project I'm working on that I could definitely use some help with. I don't want to monopolize your time, but I'm to the point where I've done all I can do with just one set of hands. I could pay you a little bit—not much—but it'll be worth your effort. What'd'ya think?"

Luke liked the idea of earning some extra cash to help cover the cost of Bessie's tow and repairs. To him, it sounded like a great offer, but maybe because it was the only one he had. "Sounds fantastic. Count me in."

7

JOLENE

J OLENE HAD EXACTLY three hours until her sister's family would arrive and approximately six hours' worth of cleaning left to do. The math didn't pencil and the house was a mess. Not by Jolene's standards, but certainly by Rose's. If the fireplace mantle didn't pass the white glove test, the house was considered a pigsty. Jolene often found it hard to believe the two women came from the same family, there were so many differences between them.

It didn't help that Rose thought all animals belonged outside, either. The first Christmas Jolene owned Ace had been an interesting one. When Rose headed to the spare bedroom to put away her luggage and get settled for her stay, only to find Ace snuggled up on the queen-sized bed as he customarily did, the shriek Rose squealed let her distaste be loudly known.

"Wolf!" she'd hollered. Immediately, Jolene and Rose's husband, Patrick, rushed to her aid, startled by the screaming from the back of the house. Rose stood in the doorframe, suitcase held up as a shield between her and

Jolene's new pet. "Jolie, why is there a *wild animal* in your bedroom?"

Ace just grunted and rolled over, bringing his paw up to his ear in what Jolene was sure was an effort to block out Rose's ignorant chatter.

"He's my dog, Rosie. His name's Ace. I've had him for about six months now."

"Your dog?" Rose's face was scrunched so tight it looked like she smelled something rancid. "Why on earth would you keep a dog in the house?"

"Because it's where he lives," Jolene had reasoned.

"And why doesn't he live in a *dog* house?" Rose questioned. "See? They make little houses specifically for these kinds of creatures."

That episode wasn't an isolated one. Every time Rose would visit and see a rogue dust bunny caught in the corner or blowing innocently across the floor, she'd turn up her nose, making sure Jolene noticed her disapproval. She'd asked Jolene if she could borrow a lint roller so many times that Jolene now left one on the guest room nightstand for her sister to use during visits. Her sister was a neat freak of the obsessive and compulsive variety, but Jolene didn't mind. She knew they had a different way of living and that was okay. People were allowed their quirks. Heaven knew Jolene had plenty of them.

✳

JOLENE WAS STILL running the vacuum when she saw the van pull into her driveway. For as opposite as they were, Jolene sure loved the time she got to spend with her sister. And now that she was an aunt, she coveted the time with her little niece, Ava. It had been six months since their last visit and that was much too long to wait for adorable baby snuggles.

Flipping the vacuum switch off and tightening her frizzy ponytail by tugging on two sections of her hair, Jolene readied herself for company. She could hear her sister and brother-in-law squabbling outside about who would bring in the playpen and she decided she needed to intervene. Traveling with an infant couldn't be easy. She felt for them and the three-hour drive they'd just embarked upon. It sounded like they could certainly use a little help.

"Welcome to Merrylark, family!" Jolene bellowed as she bounded down the steps toward the silver minivan. "How were your travels?"

Rose was in the middle of unlatching Ava from her infant carrier. She handed the towheaded baby off to her husband and looked at her sister. "Noisy. And smelly. Excruciatingly smelly."

"Ava had a blowout on highway 42," Patrick explained.

Jolene joined them in the driveway and reached over to Patrick to gather her niece from his arms. "Better than your tire having one, I suppose."

"I'm not so sure about that," Rose groaned. She pulled an enormous floral-printed diaper bag from the back seat and then clicked the automatic sliding door shut with her key fob. "For such a sweet little thing, she sure can make a terrible stink. Think skunk and decomposed fish, with a sprinkling of rotten milk. Seriously, I don't know what on earth her parents are feeding her," Rose deadpanned. Jolene was grateful her sister could make light of it all. Motherhood had unwound a little of her tight personality and that was a good thing. "She's due for a bath and I'm due for a drink."

"I think we can arrange for both," Jolene said, smiling.

Jolene followed her younger sister into the house. Patrick made several trips back to the van to collect the remaining things they would need for their stay. It was amazing what light packers the two used to be when they were childless, but now with an infant it looked like they had plans to move in. High chair, play pen, portable crib, walker. You name it, they brought it. Jolene loved it, actually. While her home always felt comfortable—cozy and warm— it lacked people, family. The sounds of laughter and life. Hers was a quiet one. Sure, she talked to Ace and sometimes he would bark out his response, but the clatter and chatter of voices was absent from her house and she missed that. Ached for it even.

"Sorry a baby store just exploded in here, Jo," Patrick said as he shut the front door behind him. He carried three stuffed animals in his arms, all various shades of pink. "I would love to say something like, 'You won't even notice us,' but we all know that's a blatant lie. We're pretty much a trav-eling circus at this point. Looks like we're moving in, not just staying two short nights."

"No apologizing, Patrick. You know I love it when you guys come to stay." Jolene squeezed her brother-in-law's arm and grabbed one of the stuffed toys to give to Ava. "I'll take any time I can get."

Patrick was a good man, the very best for her sister. Where Rose could be erratic, Patrick was consistent. They'd met in law school, fallen in love, graduated and passed the bar, and gotten married all within the span of a year. It was fast and intense, much like her sister's personality, so no less could be expected. But Patrick was level-headed and steady. He dressed smartly, gave generously, and brought Rose back down to earth when her thoughts and compulsions carried her too far off. It was wonderful to have someone like that in the family, a patriarch of sorts. Though the sisters' father had been gone for nearly fifteen years now, that void remained. Patrick was doing a great job filling it, as much as he was able to, at least. That meant the world to the Carter women.

"When's mom coming?" Rose called out from the kitchen. She had a plastic tub of baby bottle pieces that she had unpacked and then stacked on a drying mat on the counter.

"She's not." Jolene crouched onto the floor, settling Ava down next to her. She knew this was likely pushing it for her sister, what with all the invisible dog hair. Sometimes she figured it was better to ask forgiveness than permission and she'd take her chances on this one.

"Mom's not coming?" Rose froze. Her voice jumped two octaves. "Why on earth not? What could possibly be more important than her annual Christmas celebration with her only daughters?"

"An all-expense paid cruise to the Bahamas with Carl."

Patrick chuckled. "Good for Mary, that little vixen."

"One," Rose held up a finger and waggled it at her husband, "don't ever call my mom a vixen again. Gross. And two, since when am I the last to find out about our Carter Christmas plans?"

"Since you decided to stop answering your phone, I think," Jolene replied. She and her niece were playing a game of peek-a-boo behind the stuffed teddy bear and the giggles the game elicited were music to Jolene's ears. She'd gone too many months without hearing that precious laughter.

"I told you I don't use it for that." Rose let out an audible huff that bordered on a growl. "Ever heard of texting?"

"What? And miss out on this very priceless, in-person reaction?" Jolene shook her head. "No way. Don't think so."

"Girls, girls," Patrick ordered in an attempt to bring peace. The sisters weren't fighting though; they never really did. Even when they disagreed on things, it never escalated into argument territory. Jolene couldn't remember if that had always been the case or if it was something that developed after their dad's death, like a coping mechanism. Remaining a team, no matter what and against any and all odds. Whatever the reason, Jolene never took it for granted. Family was priceless, a true gift and treasure.

Rose continued to unpack in the kitchen while Patrick located the television remote between the couch cushions and flicked it on to watch a football game that came on in the third quarter. He slipped off his brown loafers, ruffled his gelled black hair, and unbuttoned the dress shirt he had been wearing so his white undershirt showed underneath. Why Rose had him dressed to the nines for a day of travel was beyond Jolene, but she wasn't really surprised by it. They were always so put together, like at any moment they were ready for a spontaneous family portrait session.

Unlike Jolene, Rose's blonde bob was sleek and professional. Her makeup was on point, from her sharp and defined brows to her perfectly penciled lips. She was petite and absolutely stunning and wore clothes tailored exactly for her body. Rose was the kind of woman who was back in her pre-maternity clothes only three weeks after giving birth. While Jolene was fit and relatively toned, she doubted her body would bounce back like that after pregnancy. She liked food way too much and if a few extra pounds were the trade-off for happiness, she'd gladly keep them around her midsection.

Back in the kitchen, after Rose had unloaded enough

luggage to feel like she could sit down to take a breather, she came over to the couch, two glasses of white wine in her slender hands. She offered one to Jolene who was still entertaining Ava on the rug.

"So what have you been up to, sis? Still tending to the O'Connell cottage?"

"Yep," Jolene answered. She took a sip of the wine and felt the cool liquid slide down her throat. Ava had started to rub her eyes with her tiny, chubby fists, a cue that naptime was on the horizon. "Still doing that."

"And working a real job yet?" Rose clearly wanted some news on Jolene's future employment plans. They all knew the money was nearly gone. Five years was as long as Patrick had figured Jolene would be able to make her savings last. From day one, he'd said she'd need to make longer-term plans. They'd penciled out a budget and Jolene had stuck to it like it was her religion. Just like the loaves and fishes, she'd hoped she'd be able to stretch it further than she knew it could possibly go. Unfortunately, a miracle was not in her cards.

"I'll find something...soon," Jolene admitted. She quickly took another swig of wine and kept it in her mouth so she didn't have to answer any other questions just yet.

"You know I only ask because I worry about you."

"I know." Jolene wasn't mad. Not even annoyed. If anything, it felt good to be loved enough that someone worried about her. "I appreciate the concern. I do. Really."

Rose smiled, her mouth curving. "Here." She waved at Ava with two flapping hands. "Give her here. I'll get her fed and put down for a nap. The back bedroom, right?"

"Yeah, but I think Ace is already back there snoozing. Let me go wake him and get him moved for you."

"I can do it."

Jolene's mouth gaped at her sister's words.

"What? Don't look so shocked." If she did appear that way, Jolene couldn't help it. "Having a baby who throws half her meal from her high chair has made me recognize the value in having an animal around to vacuum it up. Remind me to show you pictures of Winston after I put Ava down. He's an absolute doll."

Jolene was going to have to physically push her jaw back up with her hand. "Rose Carter Smith. I do believe hell hath frozen over."

"Oh yeah," Rose said, laughing over her shoulder as she walked down the hall with her daughter. "And pigs flew and there was even a blue moon or two. It's been quite a year. I'll get you all caught up. How about we grab some dessert once the hubby and the baby are down for the night and we can chat?"

"Sweets and my sister? How could I say no to that?"

"You can't," Rose hollered in a sing-song tone.

Jolene took another sip of her wine and smiled. There really was nothing like a house full of family. She wondered if she'd ever have one of her own to fill it.

8

LUKE

LUKE'S HANDS ACHED, but it felt great to use them for something worthwhile. For as monotonous as shoeing horses and mending fences had become, he was the type of man that needed to do physical work to feel satisfied. He'd never been content with idleness when it came to his body. Once, just out of high school, he'd applied for a desk job at his uncle's IT firm. Nothing about that venture went well. On his first day, he crashed their main server and also managed to lose three potential clients to a competing firm when he misspoke about the capabilities of the software he attempted to sell. To him, it was another language altogether. Getting fired by his uncle was a humbling moment, but learning he was better suited for a different sort of work was a revelation he was glad he'd made in his younger years.

Work that involved sweat, strength and muscle was right up his alley. That's why working with Devon was the perfect fit. There was physical labor to be done and Luke was a ready and willing employee.

❄

A FEW HOURS into their afternoon, Devon swept the back of his hand across his tall forehead and let out a grunt fit for a caveman. "See?" he said. "Told you it would be hard work."

"That's the best kind, though, right?" Luke answered. He set the mallet down on the windowsill and gathered his breath. "Where's the satisfaction in easy work? A night when I go to bed with my bones aching and my body weary is a day that I know I've earned every penny of my paycheck."

"Spoken like a true cowboy."

"What can I say? It's in my blood." Luke laughed heartily. "And I don't know about you, but right about now, I'd like a little something in my stomach. I'm still craving that cheesecake from Sal's we never got."

"Yeah brother, gotta be honest, I've never had a waitress neglect me that much before. It's almost like she purposefully ignored our table the entire time. Must've been intimidated by the handsome devils we so obviously are." Devon opened the lid to his aluminum toolbox and bent down on the newly installed floorboards to collect the other discarded tools.

The space was coming together nicely. Luke wasn't sure what it had looked like before, but according to Devon, the place should've been condemned. Three years ago, there had been a grease fire in the mesquite barbecue restaurant directly underneath it. Not much was salvageable. Apparently the previous owners left town with the insurance money and the property eventually went to auction. Devon and his father scooped it up, but for the better part of a year it sat vacant. Only recently had Devon been able to dedicate any substantial amount of time refurbishing the upstairs space. Renovating the old restaurant had originally been their first priority, but they had plans to flip the property as a whole, both upstairs portion and retail space below. The electrical had recently been completed and the walls sheet rocked, taped and mudded. Today, the men finished laying the rest of the hardwood flooring, making the space nearly rental ready. It was fulfilling, measurable work, Luke's favorite kind.

Dessert was also his favorite.

"I'm gonna hang around here and clean up, but if you're only in town for the week, you need to check out The Rolling Pin," Devon suggested. "My aunt owns the place. It's a little frilly for a guy's guy like yourself, but Aunt Martha's pastry case houses some of the best baked goods you'll find within a three-hundred-mile radius. This time of year the shortbread is in short supply, so I'll make a call and ask her to set some aside for you."

"I don't discriminate when it comes to sugar. Whatever she's got left is fine by me." Luke looked out the large, arched second floor window that faced Glenn Street. Townspeople lined the sidewalks with their shopping bags in hand and smiles worn brightly. He felt like he'd completed a puzzle with his grandfather back when he was a kid that had this very scene. "Point me in the right direction?"

"Down by Randy's Tree Lot. Just on the corner. You won't be able to miss it. Your nose will lead the way."

❄

"THIS ONE'S ON the house." A plump woman in what Luke figured to be her sixties said as she brought a small plate to his table and set it down in front of him. She wore her graying hair in a tight, round bun on the top of her head and it looked just like the bagels she served in her shop. The red apron tied around her neck accentuated the pinkish

glow of her cheeks and to Luke, she mirrored every illustra-
tion he'd ever seen of Mrs. Claus. He wondered how often
she got that comment. "A slice of our famous peppermint
pie. Best seller the entire month of December for twelve
years running."

"Thank you kindly, ma'am," Luke said. He rubbed
absentmindedly at his stomach, already full from the triple
fudge brownie and three macaroons he'd consumed. "But
I'm happy to pay you for it."

"Not a chance. My nephew called earlier and said you'd
be heading over so I made sure to save you a slice." The
woman patted Luke on his shoulder in a motherly way.
"And once you're finished with that, I've got some shortbread with your name on it. Just give me a holler,
sweetheart."

Luke pushed back from the table, stretching his gut.
"You'll have to roll me out of here when I'm all done."

"What do you think the big man in the back is for?" As if
on cue, a large gentleman wearing an identical apron
saluted from behind the glass pastry case. He had to be
Martha's husband because he could've been mistaken for
the man in red himself.

Luke laughed and grabbed his fork to dive in.

The Rolling Pin was a great spot. For the last half-hour,
there had been a steady stream of customers lined up to the
counter to place their holiday orders. Yet, for as successful as
the place appeared, the accommodations just weren't there.
Luke sat in one of four rectangular, two-person tables located
within the shop. Outside there were only three more, crowded
on a narrow strip of sidewalk that passersby dodged and
skirted. While he wanted to consider it quaint, he suspected
many found it to be crowded. If he scooted his chair out even

an inch, he'd bump into the person sitting directly behind him. That would've been annoying if any person other than Jolene Carter had been the one taking that seat.

"Luke?" she said in a tone threaded with both surprise and obvious delight. "I haven't seen you all day!"

The way in which she spoke nearly suggested disappointment about that fact. Luke couldn't say he didn't feel the same. While he'd originally planned to avoid Jolene—not for any other reason than wishing not to overwhelm her—she'd been close to his thoughts and mind all afternoon. Running into her at The Rolling Pin felt like a welcome, unforeseen encounter.

"Rose." Jolene held out a hand to the woman seated opposite her. "This is my neighbor, Luke. The one I was telling you about who's renting the O'Connell place for the week. Luke," she swiveled back, "this is my sister, Rose. She's here with her husband and baby for a couple of days to celebrate the holidays."

"Nice to meet you." Luke tipped his head in greeting. While each woman had her individual, unique look, he could spot the family resemblance instantly. It was evident in their dimpled cheeks and heart-shaped mouths that were tinted the same shade of raspberry red. Even though the texture of their hair was different, the hue matched almost perfectly. That they were related wouldn't come as a shock to anyone upon first introduction. They wouldn't be mistaken for twins, but certainly siblings. "You live close by?"

"Not at all. It took half a lifetime to finally get here."

"She's lying," Jolene quickly corrected, interjecting like she thought Luke might believe her sister's sarcastic words. "They're just outside of Hickoryvale."

"She's right, what I meant to say was the drive here shaved off half of my life."

"They have an eight-month-old," Jolene explained again. She twirled the straw in her milkshake between her slender fingers. Luke thought it was cute how she felt the need to interpret for her sister. "Ava's not a fan of car rides."

"I get it. My sister's got a fifteen-month-old and they live two states away. I have a feeling they won't be traveling until my nephew is at least eighteen. Last time I spoke to her, Corey was going through the *I hate being strapped into anything* phase. Don't figure that's any fun."

"I truly don't understand the problem," Jolene said. She tried to remain straight-faced, but her arched lips betrayed her. "Ava is always a perfect angel for me. I can't imagine her ever causing any amount of trouble for anyone."

Rose huffed. "I'm telling you, sis, the offer still stands. I'm leasing her out, one year at a time. Didn't I hear you say you were volunteering for the terrible twos?"

Luke enjoyed being a spectator to the sisters' friendly banter. It gave him a glimpse into yet another side of Jolene and, like every other part he'd already gotten to know, he liked this side, too. There was no pretense, no game. These were the sorts of characteristics that were hard to come by these days, even harder to find in someone single.

Not that he was going to date her. They weren't going to date. Luke made his brain take a swift detour from any road it planned to go down with that thought.

Jolene was his lake house neighbor, that was all. Temporary neighbors.

"Luke," Rose hollered around her sister, meeting Luke's eyes. "Why don't you slide your chair on over here and join us? You're looking pretty lonely all by yourself."

"Luke's not lonely," Jolene defended in a high-pitched voice. "He's perfectly fine."

"From our conversation earlier, I was already aware that you thought he was *fine*, but I'm telling you, he also looks lonely."

Martha swooped in with her promised shortbread, delivering three pieces to her customers. "And I present to you," she made a drumroll noise by stomping her feet on the tiled floor, "The Rolling Pin's signature shortbread! Merry Christmas, all. Enjoy!"

Luke swung his chair around and joined the sisters at their table, but Jolene's focus remained on her dessert. He figured if he looked at her long enough, she'd have to look up at some point. He was dying to see her reaction to her sister's confession.

"Hi," he said, grinning when her eyes finally flitted up to his. He held their connection until she blinked her thick eyelashes rapidly and dropped her eyes back down, but he noticed how she bit her bottom lip to pin back a smile. He popped a bit of cookie into his mouth, satisfied and even feeling a little confident. "This is mighty *fine* shortbread, don't you agree?"

"Oh, this one's a funny one." Rose pointed the tines of her fork toward Luke and shot him a wink. "I like him."

"Me too," Jolene said quietly and this time when she looked up at Luke, she didn't hide the smile that crept onto her lips. "Me too."

9

JOLENE

PATRICK WAS SNORING on the couch when the sisters arrived home. Though they tried to be quiet when opening and closing the front door, it always stuck in the jamb and required a hip bump to push it all the way into place. Evidently that was just enough noise to wake up a sleeping Ava in the back room, but it did nothing to rattle Patrick who continued mimicking a locomotive with his loud, gurgled breathing.

"I'll go feed Little Miss and get her settled back down," Rose said as she slipped her patchwork leather purse off of her shoulder and set it on the table in the hallway. "Might even turn in for the night myself. The drive this afternoon was an exhausting one. I'm not at all surprised Patrick's already out like a light."

"Want any help with Ava?"

"Nah. I've got it." Rose shook her head then looked over at her husband. "Okay if I leave Patrick there for now? I'm sure he'll head to bed once he wakes and realizes the football game is over, but waking that man from his hibernation is a feat I don't have the energy for at the moment."

Jolene placed her keys on a hook on the wall and slipped the wool jacket from her shoulders to hang next to them. "Of course. I'm just going to tidy up and probably turn in for the night, too." Then, taking her sister's shoulders within her hands she squeezed and said, "It's good to have you here, Rosie. Really good."

"It's good to be here, sis." Rose leaned forward and kissed her sister swiftly on the cheek. "Love you."

"Love you, too."

Jolene looked around her family room. Most everything was still in place from her earlier organizing and the mad dash to clean up before Rose got into town. There was, however, a small box of ornaments next to the fireplace that hadn't been there earlier. Jolene smiled when she realized her brother-in-law must have baby proofed the Christmas tree while they were out, as the bottom two feet were now bare, only the twinkling lights adorning their branches.

Bending down to pick up the box, she gathered it into her arms and headed outside. It was late, nearing nine-thirty, but she knew Luke was still awake, mostly because they'd given him a ride back to the O'Connell house, dropping him off only five minutes earlier. She doubted he'd settled in for the night that quickly and figured now would be a good time to catch him.

Balancing the box on her hip, she lifted her hand to knock on Luke's door, but it opened before her fist could connect with its surface.

"Jolene," Luke greeted, his teeth revealed behind a huge smile. While he hadn't gone to bed yet, he had managed to change out of his jeans and jacket and into a white V-neck shirt and plaid flannel pants. His feet were bare and Jolene had to blink her way back up to his face, trying to keep her focus there. "I leave something in your car?"

"No." Jolene shifted the box. "But I do have those ornaments I promised for your tree. I thought maybe you'd like them?"

Luke gave her a blank stare, like he was trying to figure something out about her and his pause gave Jolene just enough time to fill up with insecurity. "Never mind. It's late and you're obviously wanting to get to bed what with the pajamas and all. This could've waited until tomorrow—"

"No, no." Luke's hand shot out and touched her arm. "It's not all that late. Come on in."

Desperation was not a good look on anyone and she feared she wore hers so visibly, so plainly. She'd never wanted to come across that way, especially in front of someone like Luke. They barely knew each other and here she was forcing her hand-me-down ornaments on him when he so obviously had hopes of going to bed.

"I really should go." She spun on her heel.

"Don't." Luke's voice was firm this time, punctuated and strong. Then it softened when he said, "Please stay, Jolene. I mean it. I'd really like the company."

That drawl she loved curled around her like a hug.

Luke took the box. "Let's see what we've got here. Want to stick around and help me do a little late-night tree decorating? I could get some hot chocolate going."

Self-doubt expanded in her chest again. "See? It *is* late, Luke. I can come back in the morning—"

Setting the box down onto the floor and then straightening back up, Luke reached out for Jolene, taking her hands into his large ones. Her heart rammed in her ribcage and her throat went dry. He dipped his head down to draw her eyes up to meet his steady gaze and he intentionally held onto her so she couldn't look away.

"I want to spend more time with you and I would love it

if you would help me decorate. Right now it's just a tree and from what I've seen, you have the perfect touch to turn it into a Christmas tree. What do you say?"

Jolene could feel her cheeks warming, her palms clamming up with sweat. It was like she'd lost all knowledge of the English language. Her nodding head answered the wobbly "yes" that her mouth couldn't muster.

"Good." He dropped only one of her hands and scooped up the cardboard box. "So, let's see just what we're working with here."

Jolene followed Luke into the family room, guided by their intertwined hands. She loved where he'd chosen to place the tree—right in the middle of the room with the sprawling windows framing it in. The way things were situated, the glass barrier between the inside of the house and the outdoors barely seemed noticeable. The tree drew it all in, bringing nature into the space. While Jolene loved her own tree, it was shoved in the corner by the fireplace, hemmed in with walls on two sides. Here, Luke's was displayed in such a lovely way that she couldn't wait to get started with the decorating. It was going to be the perfect Christmas tree.

Remembering there was a box of lights used for the outside of the house stored in the hall crawl space, Jolene sent Luke to collect them while she warmed up some water on the stove for hot cocoa. Luke returned just as the teapot whistled.

"All I could find were the clear lights. These the ones you're thinking of?" Luke wrapped a strand around his upper body and twisted at the waist to playfully show them off.

"Yep," Jolene said through a giggle. "Those are them."

She brought a mug of hot chocolate over to Luke. He took it from her. "Careful, it's hot."

"Thank you, Jolene." He took a sip. "Mmm. Perfect." Unwinding the lights, he turned toward the tree. "Shall we get started?"

"We shall."

For the next hour, the two trimmed the tree. Jolene reminisced about every ornament pulled from the box. She found herself telling stories about them, not meaning to at first, but as the night went on, she noticed Luke prompting her to do so by holding up each one for her to recall.

"What about this?" Luke lifted up a pink flamingo that glittered with sequins. "There's gotta be a story behind this one."

"Oh jeez!" Jolene snatched the ornament from Luke and turned it over in her palm. "That was from my mom and Rosie about six years ago. They always teased me that I had terrible balance. *Lady Grace*, they often called me. I would argue that I had enough style to make up for my clumsiness, and apparently this ornament perfectly illustrated that, what with the flashy looking flamingo balanced on one leg and all. I still can't stand on one leg without falling over. I'm a complete klutz." She shrugged and looked wistfully out at the lake. "I don't know. I suppose it's a little silly to decorate *your* tree with all of *my* memories, isn't it?"

"I think it's perfect." Luke ducked around the tree to retrieve another ornament from the stash. "You have nice memories."

Jolene smiled. She found herself doing that whenever Luke was around, like she couldn't keep her lips from lifting into a spontaneous grin. It was so good to be happy like this again.

"This one?" An ornament of an envelope that read *Season's Greetings* dangled from his finger.

"That's from my mailman, Stan. A little self-explanatory and not all too creative, I suppose."

Luke shook his head, but not in disagreement. It came across more as a gesture of amazement. "Even your mailman gives you Christmas gifts? Jolene, is there anyone in this town whose life you haven't impacted?"

She didn't know how to answer that. If there was one thing about Jolene, it was that she never knew how to properly accept a compliment. Praise of that nature felt awkward to acknowledge. She was anything but rude, though, so she offered an unsure smile.

"Okay." Luke stepped forward and suddenly took her by the shoulders. "I can see I've made you uncomfortable, but indulge me for a minute while I make you just a little bit more uncomfortable."

Panic seized her. She had no clue what Luke was going to do. If she was honest, it felt like the place for a kiss. If it had been a movie, this was where the guy would draw the girl into his arms and plant one on her, the crescendo of an emotional scene. She found herself hoping for that just as much as she hoped he would let her go. Jolene felt caught right in the middle of her emotions, torn in two opposing directions of hesitation and yearning.

"Jolene, I'm going to teach you how to take a compliment because compliment receiving is a practice that we should all be adept in. Especially someone like you, who I would imagine receives multiple compliments a day." With a gentle hand placed on the small of her back, he guided her to the couch just a few feet away. "Here," he motioned, "Sit across from me."

She did as instructed, feeling a bit like she was a student

in class. They both folded their legs underneath them, and she wanted to laugh when Luke struggled with his long legs and big feet on the small sofa. He looked like a human pretzel.

"Two rules." Luke held up as many fingers. "You're not allowed to break eye contact and you're not allowed to disagree. All you can do is say *thank you.* Understood?"

She nodded, though her agreement didn't mean she was any less uncomfortable with the rules of the game.

"Jolene." There was that alluring drawl again. She wondered if her face gave away the way his voice made her insides melt. She swallowed. "I've only known you two days, but I can already see how amazing you are." Luke's finger came up to her face and skimmed the side of her cheek as it brushed away an errant curl. "You radiate joy and generosity. Seriously, who else would offer up half of their tree's decorations?"

"It's more like a quarter—"

Luke lifted his finger to shush her. "No talking yet, remember?" Jolene shrugged back but stopped her sentence from continuing. Luke paused, just staring at her for a moment. "You make a mean cup of coffee and an equally delicious hot cocoa, might I add. You've got some really great friends, even that old Mildred and her fourteen cats. The verdict's still out on Hank," he continued to say, laughing. "I've enjoyed spending time with you more than I can even tell you." Their eyes locked, but Luke's squinted like he was trying to work something out, trying to decipher his feelings even as he freely spoke them. "Gosh, you're so beautiful. Like, *really* beautiful." Though he sounded like a bashful schoolboy, Jolene still felt his words deep in her stomach. No man had told her she was beautiful in recent years. Hearing Luke say it did weird things to her breathing, her heart, her mind. "I think maybe I actually shouldn't be telling you any of this…" His voice trailed off and a stunned look came over his features. He pressed his palms to his thighs and quickly pushed off to stand. "I'm sorry."

He'd instructed her not to blink, but even if he hadn't, she wouldn't've been able to anyway. Her eyes remained saucers, stunned and round.

"I've said more than I should have." Turning his back to her, he faced the tree and brought his hand up to the back of his neck and rubbed it. "Let's get this finished up."

Jolene stayed folded up on the couch, but managed to squeak out a small, "Thank you," after a few moments of quiet between them.

Luke spun around. "What's that?"

"I said thank you." She uncurled her legs and walked over to the tree, which was now mostly decorated and shining brightly. "You said all I could say was *thank you*, so I'm saying it. And I mean it. Those were genuinely nice things to say about me."

Luke's mouth curved up on one side before he dropped down to dig into the box of remaining decorations. "Well, you're most welcome. So tell me about this one?"

❄

JOLENE WAS SHOCKED to hear the clock in the kitchen chime eleven. They'd finished the tree trimming just a little bit ago. At one point, Luke stopped inquiring about the ornaments and seemed to be done with the story telling. She was fine with that, as recounting all of her Christmas memories had taken more of an emotional toll than she was prepared to experience. She had planned to leave after they were done, but Luke flicked on the television without seeming to want to end their evening just yet. A holiday movie had already begun, but they easily picked up on the plot and sat together on the couch to watch, a second mug of cocoa in their hands.

It reminded Jolene of being on a date at the movies as a teenager. They both took up their own couch cushion and didn't cross over into the other's space. From the corner of her eye, she could see Luke's upturned hand on the sofa and she wanted to reach for it, but she wasn't bold in that way and, if anything, she was of the old fashioned mindset that the guy should make the first move. Maybe that's what Luke had already done when he'd told her she was beautiful, but as far as things went physically, she would wait on him. If he was even planning to make a move. She'd jumped so far ahead with that thought that her head was spinning.

Neighbors. Just neighbors.

"What are your plans tomorrow?" Jolene asked during a commercial break that Luke had used the television remote to mute. Growing up, her dad always did the same thing and that made her smile. "Anything fun?"

"I've gotta try to make it to the grocery store, for starters." Luke fiddled with the controller, turning it over in his hands.

"Betty still not working?"

"Bessie—and no, she's not, but I do know what's wrong with her, so that's a plus. Fuel pump gone bad."

"Sounds expensive." Jolene had no clue if it really was, but she just assumed anything having to do with cars was pricey to fix.

"Not too bad. A few hundred. I need to check in town to see if I can get the things I need to fix it, but it shouldn't be all that much. Could've been worse."

Jolene leaned forward to set her mug onto the coffee

table. "If you haven't been to the grocery store yet, I take it you don't have any breakfast food?"

"You're right about that. All I have are the staples in the cupboards, but I'll make do. I was thinking of mixing up a little sugar, garlic powder, and the croutons I saw in there for a hearty meal to start my day," he joked. "Maybe sprinkle a few bacon bits over the top if I'm feeling special."

"Breakfast of champions." Jolene laughed. "Listen, how about you come over at ten and join us for brunch? Roger will be there and my good friend Cat and her family. My sister, too, although I don't know if that's more of a deterrent after our awkward run-in at The Rolling Pin."

"What was awkward about it?"

"Oh, please." Jolene rolled her eyes. "My sister has a really, really big mouth. She's never been good at censoring."

"I like it. No beating around the bush. No games. I think that's a mighty *fine* way to be."

Jolene blushed instantly. "So we're not going to drop that, are we?"

Leaning in and bopping the pad of his index finger against her nose, Luke shook his head and said, "Nope. And since I admitted to thinking you're beautiful, it's only fitting that you find me mighty fine."

"Only fitting?"

Luke nodded confidently. "Yep."

"Okay, then it's only fitting that—seeing as you have no real food to speak of in this house—you join us for brunch tomorrow morning. Ten o'clock."

"I can handle that. I'd offer to bring something, but I don't have much in the way of anything to offer at the moment."

"Your presence will be enough. Perfect even."

"So now you think I'm perfect, too, is that right?"

Jolene couldn't catch a break and Luke knew it. He'd pounced on that opportunity right as the words came out.

"Ten o'clock. Sound good?"

"Ten o'clock."

"I really should go. Thanks again for the lovely evening, Luke. I've had a great time." Jolene rose from the couch and started to head toward the door. She could sense Luke's imposing body following her as she padded across the room, his chest so close to her back that she could feel his warmth on her skin. She wanted to lean back into him, to feel his solid frame against her, but that would be a crazy thing to do. Absolutely crazy.

She had her hand on the door knob to go, but Luke's palm lighted on her shoulder.

"Jolene?" She turned to look up at him, at his pale blue eyes and unsure but smiling mouth. "Thanks for coming by tonight. I know we talked a lot about your memories, but tonight it felt like we created one of our own, and I hope I'm not being too forward when I say that I'd like for it to be the beginning of many more."

"I'd like that too, Luke," Jolene said. "A lot."

It surprised her that she truly meant every word.

10

LUKE

H E HEARD THE telltale backing-up beep in his dream before it registered in reality. Sitting up, Luke shoved open the drawn bedroom curtains and saw his dear Bessie strapped and chained to the back of Hank the Ogre's truck, both vehicles leaving the driveway and turning onto Spruce Lane as one large and awkward metal unit.

Luke blinked repeatedly. The clock on the nightstand read 9:40 in red block numbers, the kind that taunted during bouts of insomnia. Right now, it mocked him over how late he'd overslept. As much as he wanted to race out into the cold December air and flag down Hank and his beloved Bessie, he couldn't be late for Jolene's invitation to brunch. He doubted Hank was up to anything questionable. In such a small town, Luke figured he'd catch wind of it if he was. He would deal with Bessie later, once he had a clearer head and a full belly.

He rinsed off quickly in the shower and threw on a pair of worn jeans and his favorite green and blue plaid flannel, which bore an embarrassing resemblance to the lake house's living room couch. He wondered if Jolene would notice. If she did, she'd probably just rib him about it a little, which would be deserved after the way he'd teased her the night before. He didn't know why he'd brought up what she had said about him at the café. Maybe it was his way of confirming his feelings weren't one-sided. Though she was friendly and even at times flirty, Luke couldn't tell if Jolene experienced the same connection that he felt between them. He worried he was reading into it all, seeing and feeling things that weren't even there.

Scrubbing a toothbrush over his teeth, he looked himself squarely in the mirror.

"Handley, you're not an awkward twelve-year-old boy. Grow up and just ask her out."

He glanced over his shoulder at the reflection of the bedside clock which read 00:01 in backward numbers. Tossing his toothbrush to the counter, he left the bathroom and hurried down the hall, grabbing his jacket from the coat rack in the entryway on his way out the front door. Merrylark's winter smacked him in the face like a slap from a cold, icy hand. The walk over was short and Luke only had one arm in his coat sleeve when Rose opened the front door to greet him.

"Morning Luke," Rose said as she wrung her hands in a flour sack towel with an embroidered Santa Claus on it. "Glad you could make it. Come on in." She shot out a free hand and wiggled her fingers. "Here, let me take your coat that you're not even really wearing."

"Thank you kindly, Rose." Luke shrugged out of his half-on jacket.

"Is that Cool Handley Luke I hear?" a quivering voice hollered from behind Jolene's sister. Roger Wilkins shuffled into the entryway, back rounded and head low. He had brown loafers on and a navy cardigan that was just a shade lighter than his slacks. "Thought so. How the heck are you, son?"

"Not half bad, Roger. Not half bad. Yourself?"

Roger took Luke's hand into his grip for a firm shake. "Well, the good Lord gave me the blessing of another day, and for that, I can't complain."

"What's the hold up in the hallway?" Jolene's sing-song voice seized Luke's attention instantly. "Oh." She stopped in her tracks and a smile burst onto her face. She always looked half-surprised, half-delighted to see him. "Luke! I'm really glad you could make it."

"Morning, Jolene." Their eyes met and at that moment, it was only the two of them in the entryway. At least for Luke. Everyone else faded into the walls, the décor, the background noise that suddenly muted like last night's commercials, leaving only Jolene's words ringing in his ears. "Appreciate the invite."

"So I hear you have a proper Christmas tree now, compliments of my baby-proofing." A man about Luke's age shoved his way into the hallway, congregating in the small space at the front of Jolene's home. "I'm glad Ava's obsession with grabbing everything within arm's reach managed to benefit someone. Seems to only make our lives more difficult," he said with a wink added on. "Hi there. I'm Patrick, Rose's husband."

"Luke Handley," Luke introduced. "I do have to say, my tree certainly looks a lot better thanks to you."

"He's not lying," Jolene agreed. "We should all take a trip on over to admire it after our brunch. Tonight's tree for the town lighting has nothing on Luke's masterpiece."

"Buns are burning!" Someone suddenly called out from the kitchen in unison with the trill of a smoke detector that sounded like a train whistle in the confined space. "Jolene, your buns are burning!"

Jolene wrapped her fingers around Luke's forearm. It was almost like he could feel each individual finger, his nerves right on the surface of his skin, alive and electric. "I should go deal with that. I'll catch up with you in a few. Feel free to introduce yourself to those you don't know yet." She paused and flashed him another grin. "I'm really glad you could make it, Luke."

Luke was about to offer his help when he was swept into the living room by Rose's guiding hand on his elbow. "Cat, you met Luke Handley yet? Jojo's neighbor for the week, staying at the O'Connell place?"

A woman with jet black hair and winged eyeliner sized Luke up with an appreciative, sweeping head-to-toe once over. "Don't believe I have. Name's Catherine but call me Cat or Kitty or anything you like, just don't call me late for dinner. This is Tanner and that old lump over there watching the game is Vick." Vick's hand shot up in a wave over the back of the couch. "We own the only coffee truck in town. Might've seen it. *Cat's Coffee Cart?* Ring a bell?"

Luke hadn't ventured out enough to be able to properly recognize storefronts or vehicles and he felt a little bad about that. The truck was obviously Cat's pride and joy.

"Got a big ol' fat orange tabby painted on the side drinking out of a pink coffee mug? No?" Cat pressed a hand on Luke's right shoulder. "Looks like I have a huge marketing fail on my hands."

"In fairness, Luke just came into town a few days ago, Cat," Rose offered.

"True, true. But we'll be out at the tree lighting this evening, so if after tonight you still don't recognize my big ol' bus, I will most definitely be taking some offense to that.

Especially considering the sizable down payment I had to make on it. And all the money on repairs I've recently sunk into it."

Luke swallowed, uncertain how to read Cat's assertiveness.

"I'm only kidding, Luke," Cat cackled. A teenage boy who Luke assumed was her son came up beside her. He was holding a baby and Luke put two and two together to figure out it must've been Rose and Patrick's daughter, Ava. Wasn't too hard to decipher who was who in such a small town.

"Mom's personality is just about as bold as her coffee," Tanner offered as an explanation. He dodged Ava's small hands that reached up to bat at his protruding ears. "Don't take anything she says too seriously."

"Oh, son." Cat ruffled Tanner's dark hair with her knuckles. "Mother knows best, right?"

"Sure, Mom," Tanner relented with a laugh. "Whatever you say."

While Jolene was open and honest, Cat was forward and direct, and Luke noticed the not-so-subtle difference. It was strange how the delivery of words—the way one's body moved while saying them, the inflection and tone and volume—all worked together to create a personality. Luke liked Cat's, but not in the same way he liked Jolene's. It made him aware how uncommon it was to really click with someone so instantly, liking absolutely everything about them.

"You coming to the lighting tonight?" Cat asked, changing the subject as she sat down next to her husband on the couch.

"I wasn't aware there was one, but it sounds like something I wouldn't want to miss."

"You're so right about that." The sound of Jolene's voice

at Luke's back made him swivel on his heels so he could look at her. "The burnt bun catastrophe has officially been handled."

"Good to hear," Luke said. "So tell me about this tree lighting."

"It's pretty much the most amazing thing ever."

"Well then, how could I miss it?"

Cat interjected, "You can't. Mostly because I'll need you to help Jojo and I work the coffee cart. I'm short again tonight. Scotty's got appendicitis or ruptured gallbladder or some other organ that's not at all cooperating with his body."

Luke raised a brow toward Jolene.

"You don't have to help, Luke. But I should. There's no way Cat can manage on her own. No one likes to watch a tree lighting without a steaming hot beverage in their hands, so that means we'll be serving them up for most of the evening."

"If that's where you plan to be, then that's where I'll be."

Cat rotated away from the conversation, but her waggling eyebrows hinted that she picked up on the obvious flirtation in Luke's words. Whether or not Jolene caught on was a different story. Luke felt this sort of pressure to make his intentions known, the one-week timeline staring him down. He liked Jolene. It was that plain, that simple.

But at the same time, things never felt more complicated.

❄

BRUNCH WAS DELICIOUS, even the burnt buns which Luke thought were just the right amount of crunchy and toasted. It was one of those shared meals where multiple conversations took place at once, like a radio dial picking up other signals, combining them all into one white-noise blur. Luke couldn't zero in on any particular discussion, so rather than joining in, he busied himself with his utensils and the food on the plate in front of him. He raked at a glob of raspberry jelly with the fork tines and every few minutes he'd look up and catch Jolene's eye from across the large, oval dining table and she'd smile sweetly at him while continuing in conversation with the person to her right or to her left. Those brief, little connections did something to Luke. Even though his stomach was full from a hearty breakfast, it felt light—hollow almost. It trembled with the flutter of nerves like he was a teenager on his first date with a girl he'd been pining after since kindergarten. He couldn't marshal his reactions and in all honesty, that aggravated him a little.

"Mark would've loved this, Jolie. Absolutely loved it." Though the conversations jumbled around him, Luke pulled out those distinct words without any trouble. Jolene's sister angled her mimosa to her lips to pull in a swallow.

Jolene didn't reply but her demeanor shifted like a sudden change in the wind. Gone was the jovial expression. Her eyes were now downcast, her brow worried and tight.

"I'm sorry, sis," Rose retracted. She settled her glass down and took up her sister's hands. Luke tried to conceal his eavesdropping. He brought his mug to his mouth and hid behind it as he studied their exchange from across the table. "I just can't believe it's been five years already. *Five years.*"

"I can believe it," was all Jolene offered. She tugged her hands back and pulled in a deep breath, then pushed off from the table. "I'm going to get the kitchen cleaned up."

Rose's eyes instantly darted to Luke. It felt like an

attempt to tell him something, but Luke didn't know what. All he knew to do was follow after Jolene.

When he rounded the corner and caught sight of her upper half doubled over the kitchen sink, her shoulders wracked in a silent sob she fought so hard to conceal back at the table, he couldn't keep his feet planted. He raced over to her. His hands grasped onto her shoulders to rotate her into his chest. It was all one motion and it was all instinct—to draw her into him like he could somehow absorb just a bit of the pain. Drain it from her and take it for himself.

She didn't protest. She folded herself within his big body and pressed her tear slicked cheek to his shirt, burying her nose against the soft, flannel fabric. Luke's chin rested on the crown of her hair and he smoothed her wayward curls with his palm. He didn't know how to properly console someone. He doubted he was even doing a decent job of it. But there was this innate need to be there for Jolene in this way at this moment. He'd never felt that pull before. Even with Kiara, he'd never been one to offer comfort. But Kiara also wasn't the type of woman who ever required it. She was tough as nails and even if something had bothered her, pride never allowed her to open up enough to receive comfort in that way.

Jolene was different. Everything about the way she clung to Luke—the way she let herself fall apart and then be gathered up in his arms—hinted at the extreme vulnerability he'd sensed in her from day one. She was expressive in her joy, but also in her pain, and that did something to Luke. The moisture that seeped into his eyes, requiring strong and deliberate blinks to push back, surprised him. Scared him.

She scared him, and what his heart felt so suddenly and so intensely toward this woman scared him more than everything else combined. Terrified him.

"I'm so sorry," she whispered suddenly against his neck. Her breath was warm, yet it made Luke shiver still. "I'm so sorry to lose it like this in front of you."

"Don't be." Luke thumbed at the single tear left on her cheek. "You don't have to apologize, Jolene."

She pushed off and swiped her nose with the back of her hand. Her body had slowed in its shaking, her tears drying and her breathing now back on track. She sniffed and shook her head before saying, "Mark was my fiancé, but I'm sure you've already pieced that together. He died five years ago today. I thought I would be okay. Time heals all wounds, right? But today was just harder than I expected. It's okay, though. I'll be fine."

"Time doesn't heal the wounds. Sometimes it just turns them into scars."

Jolene's mouth half-smiled. "Yeah, maybe. But scars make us stronger, right?"

Luke wasn't sure about that, so he didn't answer.

"Anyway, I need to get the kitchen cleaned up and you've probably got a truck to tend to—"

He touched her wrist. "Nothing I've got going on is more important than making sure you're okay."

A look of shock swept over Jolene's face. It took a second to dissolve and when she recovered, it was replaced with an appreciative smile, the one she always seemed to have reserved for him. "You're one of the good ones, Luke." She put her hand on his forearm.

"I'm not so sure about that."

"I am sure of it," she answered with enough confidence that it made Luke almost believe it for himself. "Absolutely sure."

11

JOLENE

"IT LOOKS LIKE a porcupine."

"I don't think it looks like a porcupine at all." Jolene squinted. "Maybe a pinecone. Or possibly a piece of fried chicken. Like a leg or a thigh."

"But not a snowflake? You don't think it could pass for a snowflake?" Luke cocked his head and stared into the crafted foam design in the drink he held. He slipped a sleeve onto the cup and scrunched up his nose.

"Sure. It could pass for a snowflake. Absolutely."

"You're a terrible liar, Jo."

Hearing Luke call her by a nickname made Jolene's heart do a double take.

"This is so much harder than it looks on T.V." Luke leaned his upper body through the open pickup window. "Vanilla latte for Carol!"

"You watch a lot of latte foam design shows?"

"Cake decorating is my show of choice, if you must know." He passed off the drink to the customer on the other side of the window and pulled himself back into the truck.

"But either way, it's food art, which apparently I'm terrible at it."

"Not terrible." Jolene shrugged. "Just not very good."

Luke's fingers jutted out to jab Jolene in the stomach. She tried to recoil, but fumbled, her backside bumping into the counter behind her. Plastic lids cascaded like a waterfall onto the floor of the food truck.

"Those are fighting words." Luke playfully reached out for her again. At that same moment, Cat not-so-playfully cracked his backside with the whip of the towel she'd had tucked into her apron.

"Get back to work, lovebirds."

Like they'd been caught by their parents, the two stood stick-straight, soldiers called to attention.

"Oh, come on." Cat rolled her eyes. "Are we really pretending we're oblivious to the obvious flirtatious tension in this truck? I'm surprised you can even make your way around, it's so darn thick. I bump straight into it any time I try to move around in here."

Luke spun toward the order window in an about-face. "Next! Hey there, step right up. What can I get you?"

"We're not flirting," Jolene murmured into Cat's ear. She kept her gaze trained on Luke, hoping he couldn't hear the exchange taking place just a few feet away. The way he quickly jumped to help the next customer led her to believe he didn't want to acknowledge the truth in Cat's words, either.

"If it makes you feel better to lie to yourself, then by all means, do so. But I'm not one for lying, nor am I one for letting two full grown adults who so obviously like one another behave like shy school children. This is the twenty-first century, Jo. Ask him out already."

"I'm not asking him out!" Jolene whisper-screamed. She

was certain the tenth customer in line could heard her declaration. "I am *not* asking him out," she repeated, much softer the second time. "He's only in town for a few days anyway. It wouldn't make any sense."

"A few days is more than enough time to fall in love. Vick and I were engaged after forty-eight hours and our love story is one for the books."

Jolene fiddled with a sleeve of cardboard cups. "Looks like you might need to order more smalls."

"Okay, okay. I can see you're trying to change the subject so I'll drop it. For *now*. But you've only got a few days left, Jo. Make your move before you lose your chance altogether. Luke's not the type of man you want to let get away. I'm sure he has a line of women longer than the one outside the coffee truck lined up and ready to date him. You snooze, you lose."

"You only have a few cups left. Your customers are going to be so upset if they can't order your signature small spiced latte."

"Alright, alright. I get the hint, but get back to work, or I might just dock your nonexistent pay."

❄

"I HAD NO idea latte art was so taxing. I'm exhausted." Luke rolled his shoulders and rubbed at his neck.

"This from the man who essentially runs an entire ranch back home."

"That's a kind of tired where I can feel every muscle and bone in my body. Creative work is different, and I gotta admit, I don't think I have a creative bone in my body to speak of."

"Which would make it pretty difficult for it to be tired then," Jolene said, playing off of his statement.

"I get it," he said, his eyes twinkling in a smile. He bumped her shoulder with his. "Good one."

The smell of Christmas swirled around them as they walked, the spicy aroma of the season packaged in cinnamon and pine and eggnog and cloves. There were children bundled in their puffiest jackets, which made them waddle down the sidewalk like little ducklings. Though she'd never been a mother, Jolene felt that maternal warmth in her heart just looking at them.

At the end of the roped off street, Gary and Martha Crawley were dressed as Santa and Mrs. Claus and they seated themselves on a big red velvet covered bench, as they did every year. They collected wishes and Christmas letters and made promises only Jolly Old Saint Nick himself could keep. Though it was the same scene every winter, each year it felt new to Jolene. That was the meaning of hope: the promise of new beginnings and fresh starts even amidst tradition and routines.

Some people equated the season of winter with a time of stagnation where the landscape shriveled and nature remained in a period of waiting until spring arrived with new buds and blossoms. But to Jolene, winter couldn't mean that. She'd lost everything one winter five years ago and she had to cling to the notion that this season truly did give more than it took away.

All she had to do was think back to a baby born in a manger one winter's night to turn it all into a hopeful perspective.

At her side, Luke breathed into his hands and rubbed his palms together. Jolene liked the jacket he wore tonight which was a thick, tan canvas fabric. The elbows were patched with swatches of leather and there was a rugged texture that gave it that old-time cowboy look, like the kind she'd seen in sepia-toned western movies as a young girl. She bet that jacket kept him warm on bitter nights while he rounded up his mustangs and, for an instant, Jolene wished she could join him on such an excursion, just to see what life was like from Luke's perspective. But she'd never even sat on the back of a horse before, her fear of the animal too great. She wondered if she'd be able to muster the guts to tell him that. Would he laugh? Would she realize just how different their lives were and head back home even sooner? That wasn't something she was willing to risk.

"What time's the tree lighting?" Luke spoke, snapping her from her reverie.

"Six-thirty," she replied as she glanced at her watch. "Just about ten minutes from now."

"Then it looks like we've got some time to spare." Without warning, Luke's fingers wrapped around Jolene's elbow and guided her through the throng of gatherers at the base of the majestic, enormous evergreen tree. "I've got a little something I'd like to do first."

Before Jolene could protest, she found herself next in line to sit on Santa's lap.

"Mind if I go first?" She couldn't understand what business a grown man would have asking a pretend Santa Claus for an answered wish, but there was an endearing, hopeful note in his voice and a sparkle of anticipation in his eye that she couldn't ignore.

"Please do. Be my guest."

Luke had a bounce in his step as he walked up to the bench. Martha and Gary slid apart to allow Luke to wedge himself between them, Martha gathering her billowing crimson skirt as she scooted over to offer more room. Jolene knew she was eavesdropping, but she couldn't pull her gaze from the man in front of her. She admired the way he interacted with strangers as though they were long time friends. He had such a polite and respectful air about him and it couldn't go unnoticed. The way he'd behaved this morning when she fell apart in her kitchen solidified it all for her; Luke Handley was a gentleman, a sort of rare breed she'd thought had all but gone extinct.

Even while Luke whispered his wish close to Santa Gary's ear, he kept his eyes solidly fixed on Jolene. There was a moment exchanged between them that even the sudden flash of light from the tree illuminating with thousands of twinkling bulbs couldn't pull Jolene's attention from. While hoops and hollers chorused around her, all she could hear was her heart pounding in her ears, the echo of it beating like a hundred horses stampeding down a desert valley. Just looking into Luke's eyes did that to her.

As soon as Luke's Christmas wish had been made, Gary's left eye scrunched into a wink obviously intended for Jolene. She didn't have a clue what Luke's request could be, but there was no denying it had to do with her. Her stomach felt tight, her mouth dry like it was stuffed with a dozen cotton balls.

Luke clamped a palm onto Gary's shoulder and gave it a cordial squeeze and then he turned to do a sort of half-bow as a "thank you" to Martha. Her cheeks were already rosy from a heavily coated rouge, but they deepened even more in intensity. Then he walked toward Jolene, beaming.

"What did you wish for?" she asked.

"That's not how it works."

"Sure it is. You make a wish and then you tell the first person you see, just to make sure it sticks."

"That so?" Luke's head cocked as he looked down at

Jolene. His blue eyes held hers for longer than necessary. "Some sort of Merrylark magic?"

"Absolutely. This place is full of it."

Luke grinned. "I don't doubt it is." He paused for a moment, then said with regret in his voice, "Looks like we missed the lighting."

"It's pretty hard to miss when it's about a thousand kilowatts bright. Pretty sure I'm getting a sunburn from it right now, actually."

"A thousand kilowatts, you really think so?"

"I honestly couldn't even tell you what a kilowatt is. I just thought I might be able to impress you with some fancy language."

"First of all, not sure *kilowatt* is considered fancy. Pretty sure it's in the same category as *slog*."

Jolene slapped her hand to her face and peeked out behind her gloved fingers, feigning humiliation.

"Secondly, I think a thousand kilowatts is actually a megawatt."

"Well, aren't you the fancy one now?"

"No one's ever accused me of that before," Luke joked. "And you don't have to try to impress me, Jolene. Already checked that off of the list the very first moment we met." He reached up and pulled her hands from her eyes, gave one of them a light squeeze, and then swiftly let go. "Wait a second...is that a horse drawn carriage?" Luke stood up on his toes to see over the top of the crowd, his attention instantly averted. "You have horses in this little town and you didn't bother telling me?"

Up to that point, Jolene had forgotten all about the Christmas carriages and their snowy ride around the square. It hadn't been part of her yearly tree-lighting tradition, so she'd let it slip from her memory. It was funny how the mind did that—clung to the familiar and important things and shed the rest, wheat from the chaff. Even though the carriages weren't on Jolene's radar, it didn't mean they weren't wildly popular among the rest of Merrylark's population. A decent line strung out behind Thomas O'Reilly and his regal pair of Clydesdales. The carriage business had been passed down in his family and just last year his father, Milton O'Reilly, was forced into early retirement, Alzheimer's stealing not only his memory, but his ability to drive the team of horses. That left the Christmas tradition to his eldest son. Thomas was better suited for work behind a desk than at the reins, but he was determined to make his father proud and carry on his Christmas legacy.

"We *have* to go for a carriage ride, Jolene. It wouldn't be Christmas without one."

She wanted to tell Luke she'd had many Christmases that didn't involve horses, but it was a moot point. Just as he had done earlier, he pulled her toward his destination, leading the way with a confidence Jolene found undeniably attractive.

"Is that Mildred and Roger?" Luke nudged his head forward. "Think they'd like to join us? I'd love to hear more about those fourteen cats of hers. Are they all rescues?"

Roger and Millie stood next in line. Millie was a fashion faux pas in tangible form. Atop her head of crisp white curls was a green knit hat, adorned with three larger than life poinsettias that made the hat off-kilter with the unbalanced weight. Her mouth was a matted ruby red, the deep crevices of her skin creating lines that bled lip color out from her upper lip, all feathery and smudged. She wore two wool coats, both of equal weight, and her spindly legs fashioned the loudest printed leggings Jolene had ever seen.

She looked utterly fantastic.

"JoJo, my dear." Roger's weak, yet still sweet, voice always made her heart swell. "Luke. You two youngins plan on taking a little midnight sleigh ride?"

Jolene flipped her wrist around to look at the face of her watch. "Midnight? It's barely 6:45, Roger."

"Roger's only up at midnight when his bladder wakes him to relieve it." Mildred was her usual crass self tonight, as could be predicted. "We all know I'm keeping him out way past his bedtime."

"And I'm loving every minute of it, you night owl, you." Roger jostled Mildred with a shoulder bump and though she almost missed it, Jolene thought she glimpsed the ever so slight upturn of Mildred's mouth. "Would it embarrass you all too much to take a ride with a couple of old timers like ourselves? We'd love the company if you'd be willing to grant it."

"That's exactly what we were hoping to do," Luke replied without waiting for Jolene's response.

Wishing she'd spontaneously developed the gift of telepathy, Jolene shot Luke a wary look. Now wouldn't be the best time to confess her deep-rooted fear of all things equine—not when he appeared so pleased to have her at his side and when Roger was already waiting and holding out a hand to guide her toward the carriage seat.

No, now wasn't the time.

The time would've been back when Luke had first announced he was a full-fledged cowboy. The problem was, he hadn't really announced it. It was one of those facts that just wedged itself slyly into their conversation, two days deep when she'd already found herself wanting to impress him for reasons unbeknownst to her. Now she was in the weird territory of attempting to appear impressive, to the point of using scientific measurements she didn't even know the meaning of. Now would be the time to confess to an allergy or a common phobia like arachno or claustro. Equinophobia likely wasn't even a real thing, and not one she cared to fess up about.

"Come on up," Thomas O'Reilly said, not looking any more confident than Jolene felt. That did little to loosen the tight ball in her throat. "You two take the rear." He pointed to Roger and Millie. "You take the front. Blankets are folded on the seats."

Jolene grasped onto the rails of the carriage. Even with her gloves covering them, she knew the whites of her knuckles were pushing through her skin, she held on so tightly. With a guiding hand on her hip, Luke helped hoist her into the open-air carriage. Once up, Jolene dropped into her seat like a sack of potatoes. A sack of panicked, terrified potatoes.

"You okay?"

"Mmm hmm. Yes, of course." Her breath billowed out in front of her mouth, hanging in a frosty mist in the December night's air. She wished she could be swallowed up in it; to disappear in a cloud of smoke and skip out on this grand, scary adventure. *Poof!* "I'm just great."

"You sure?"

"Yes, completely." Jolene pinched her eyes shut. She pretended not to notice the pair of fifteen hundred pound animals immediately in front of her. She had a difficult enough time trusting the engine in her car to get her from Point A to Point B, and the engine didn't even have a mind of its own. It was a machine, programmed for its job and purpose.

What if these two mammoth-sized animals decided they didn't want to give one more silent, calm sleigh ride? What if this was the time of their planned revolt? Sure, she knew it was an absurd thought, but fears were often absurd. That was what made them so scary—the way the mind could twist out the *what-ifs* into valid, possible realities.

Luke leaned in. "You're sweating, Jolene."

"It's kinda hot out, isn't it? Does anyone else feel like it's suddenly a bit hot? Like a rare winter heat wave or something?"

Mildred answered, "It's twenty-three degrees."

"My jacket must be really, really warm." The excuse was thin, but Jolene clung to it. "I believe it's one of those sub-zero types where you could be left in a snowstorm or blizzard and still be all nice and cozy. I think it's the preferred jacket of Olympic skiers, if I remember correctly. I'm pretty sure one of them even endorsed it, like they got some sort of sponsorship out of it or something. I think I saw their picture at the store where I got it, those big cardboard cutouts, you know?"

"Sounds like a bunch of hogwash if you ask me." There Mildred was again with her unsolicited opinions.

Luke flipped over his hand and pressed the flat back of it to Jolene's forehead. She shrugged back into her seat to reclaim her space. "Just wanted to make sure you weren't coming down with something," he said quietly. "You do look a little pale."

"That's just a new foundation I'm trying out. The gal at the makeup counter recommended getting two shades lighter for winter. Something about a new trend. Pale is the new tan, right?"

Luke's mouth crept into the sweetest grin. Jolene wasn't fooling anyone, but she appreciated the fact that he didn't continue pressing her on it.

Closing her eyes again, Jolene pulled in a stinging breath. Cold air infiltrated her lungs. She held it there a moment—tight and burning—then released just as the horses jostled into motion, the carriage lagging a few seconds behind. Her eyes flew open with the jerky movement.

In the same instant, Luke's hand came down over Jolene's knee in a small, silent gesture. But it wasn't small to Jolene. It was the dropped anchor on a boat about to capsize from thirty-foot swells. It was the answer to a distress call, the reply to an S.O.S. It was safety in the eye of her crazy, fictitious storm.

The large beasts lumbered forward at a walk. Jolene trained her ears to focus on the bells wreathed around their necks and the jingle that rang out with each step. If she could pretend it was Santa's sleigh—if she could adopt that notion of magic in this very moment—then she wouldn't be so afraid.

But she felt her knee tremble, knowing Luke could sense it, too.

"Here. Put this on." Unfolding the heather gray blanket with one hand, he kept the other on her leg. "I know that's an impressively warm jacket, but it doesn't quite cover your legs. They still might be a little cold."

"Thank you." She meant it as just a reply to this thoughtful gesture, but there was so much more threaded into those two words. Her head thanked Luke for his kindness, but her heart thanked him for the gift he'd given her at a time in her life when she'd felt so alone, so isolated.

The gift of his company and friendship, such a welcome, early Christmas present. That present made her warmer than any winter blanket ever could.

12

LUKE

LUKE KNEW SOMETHING was off immediately. It was amazing how in tune he was to it. For the first few minutes of the ride he tried to ignore it, tried to convince himself that he was thinking or feeling something that wasn't really there. But he couldn't keep that up. Every step, the horses confirmed what he already knew.

"Sir?" He leaned forward on the bench. He didn't want to, but he had to take his hand off of Jolene's knee. "Sir? Would you mind stopping the carriage for a minute?"

Jolene looked like she was about to be sick. The whites of her eyes were as bright as the snow around them and her pallor had taken on a greenish hue, not unlike the tree back at the square.

"Sir?"

"Thomas O'Reilly!" Mildred cackled from the back. The horses halted instantly, causing the carriage to lurch wildly forward.

Luke swung down from the carriage, his feet thudding against the icy ground. "Sir, I think your horse is lame."

"Lame?" Thomas repeated, gaping. "Which one?"

Slowly, Luke approached the horse in question on the left, placing his hand on the high, arched wither. Almost instantly, the horse's entire frame relaxed under his gentle touch, like he had healing powers pulsing through his fingertips. "I thought maybe he just took a wrong step back there, but he's head bobbing and he's pulling his right front. I don't think it's a good idea to keep him working, not with an injury like this and all the ice on the ground. What's this big guy's name?"

"Cyprus. That one's Cyprus," Thomas said in a quivering tone. He switched the reins from one hand to two.

"Hey there, Cyprus." Luke bracketed the horse's face with his two palms on its cheeks and brought their foreheads together in greeting. "I'm sorry you're not feeling well, buddy. That can't be comfortable at all now, can it?" He looked up at Thomas at the helm. "Your stable near here?"

"Less than a quarter mile west." Thomas pointed in the indicated direction. "Off Fern Road, behind the old church."

"You mind if I unhook him so Jolene and I can walk him back? I really don't think he's up for any more rides tonight. Best to let him rest up until we have a better idea as to what's wrong."

"Not at all, not at all. You seem to have a much better mind for these animals than I do. This is my first year running the business and looks like I'm not quite as cut out for it as I hoped I would be."

"Nah, you're doing just great." With his fingertips, Luke scratched behind Cyprus's fuzzy ear. "Sometimes they're perfectly fine one day and then the next they come up dead lame. Horses are funny creatures that way. But I would feel better if we got him back to the barn and stalled up so I can take a look at him and see what might be bothering him. It's likely nothing, but not a good idea to chance it."

Thomas was a man with a permanently worried look, but in that moment, relief relaxed his features. It was as though he was a student and his teacher had just said the class final had been cancelled. "That would be incredibly kind of you. But do you think Clara is strong enough to pull the carriage on her own? I've never driven with just one horse. Not sure I know how."

"She's more than strong enough. That's what these horses are bred for and I'm sure she knows the way. But I am going to have to unhook Cyprus and get the carriage rigged up for just her. Clara can finish up this ride no problem, though I wouldn't do too many more tonight. Best to call it an evening after Millie and Roger are all done."

Luke made quick work with the horses, untacking Cyprus and fitting a halter onto his long, angular face. Though his attention was fixed on the animals, there was a part of him focused on Jolene, too. He'd sensed her hesitation the moment he pointed out the carriage rides. Cyprus was lame, that was certain, but the chance to give Jolene an out and cut short their ride was a welcome opportunity. The last thing he wanted was to make her uncomfortable, especially after she'd gone out of her way to make sure his Merrylark stay was as comfortable as possible. Ending their excursion early was best for all involved. Plus, if he'd read the situation correctly, he figured Roger wouldn't mind a little extra one-on-one time with Mildred.

For Luke, it felt good to be needed in this way—to diagnose a problem and find a quick solution. His mother always joked that men were problem solvers by nature, that it was twisted into their DNA. He didn't doubt that there was something deep inside a man that made him fit for this sort of work. The small swell of pride Luke felt expanding in his chest was confirmation of his mother's lifelong assertion.

And the soft look of adoration from Jolene was just the icing on the cake. He'd be fooling himself if he said he wasn't attempting to impress her. Of course he was. But not in the way he used to try to impress women. Not like back in his younger days when he would race his lifted truck down the only main drag in town, just hoping one of the craning necks on the sidewalk belonged to a beautiful blonde girl. Or back when he and his buddies would try to outdo one another by stuffing down a few dozen spicy hot wings before succumbing to a pitcher of milk to calm the burn.

He'd learned over the passage of time there was very little impressive about juvenile acts of stupidity.

Acts of chivalry, though, that was different. Not that he was being incredibly chivalrous now; he wouldn't go nearly that far. But doing something that actually meant something—something that took a bad situation and made it better—that was worthy and downright impressive.

"Why don't you hop down and we'll take Ol' Cyprus here back to the barn?" With his free hand, Luke reached up for Jolene's. He wanted to keep their fingers intertwined but she dropped their grip the moment her boots safely touched the earth below. It wouldn't have offended him if it was just that, but the two-foot sidestep she took to put additional space between them couldn't go unnoticed. Luke recognized it, and he didn't like it.

His brow scrunched. "You okay?"

"Yep."

It was a lie, thick and blatant, even in that short little word.

"You sure?" he pressed. That added an extra twelve-inch gap in their proximity.

Luke's shoulders fell, his hopes right along with them. He looked over Cyprus's long back up toward Thomas.

"You're all good to go. We'll take Cyprus from here and meet you back at the barn."

"This is all so very much appreciated," Thomas said, a few words catching on a stutter. "I'm not sure how it is that you came to Merrylark, but I, for one, am certainly glad you did."

Thomas's appreciation, although nice, was not what Luke had hoped to gain.

The first few hundred feet of their walk was noticeably quiet. Luke's ear tuned into the uneven clopping of Cyprus's hooves, just further confirmation that the poor animal was ailing. Horses came up lame at the ranch from time to time and the telltale sound of an offbeat gait was like a siren warning to Luke. He could read so much in it, could decipher the problem and know just how to approach the solution.

He couldn't do the same with Jolene.

Something had turned offbeat between them, but Luke's heart wasn't in tune to what that something might be.

Luke wanted to address the silence, but each time his mouth opened to speak, the words were trapped, like there were too many in it, all competing to come out but none knowing in which order to do so. He figured anything he did attempt to say would be jumbled and nonsensical because that was the current state of his muddled brain, and in truth, his heart, too.

"It's not too much farther up this road." Jolene finally breached the forced quiet. "We'll make a left at that tree and you'll be able to see it. Almost there."

"Great," was all he could form.

Cyprus's labored stride worsened with every step and Luke welcomed the idea that they could get him stalled soon. It was never good to press an animal to walk when it clearly pained him to do so. But Cyprus was as stoic a horse as Luke had ever met. Some creatures were just like that. They had this uncanny ability to perform through the pain. Do what was required of them despite it being uncomfortable.

At that moment, Luke wondered if that was what Jolene had been doing this entire day. He knew it was a painful one for her and while she'd freely released her emotions that morning, she hadn't opened up anymore about this anniversary or how it made her feel. He contemplated bringing it up, but that sort of conversation wasn't one he knew how to start.

"That's it," Jolene said, nudging her nose forward. "See that little glowing light from the barn? That's where we're headed."

Like Cyprus could sense their close proximity to home and the promise of relief, he quickened his pace, pulling against the lead rope in Luke's grip and tossing his broad head up and down.

Jolene froze.

"You okay?"

She stood stark still.

"Jolene, what is it?"

Cyprus tugged again, to the point of rearing. His front hooves lifted from the ground and bits of snow fell from his feathered legs as he stomped back onto the earth. Jolene paled.

"Luke, I'm absolutely terrified—"

"What Jolene? What is it?"

"I'm terrified of—" She stopped short again and then her chest expanded with a huge breath. "Horses."

Now it was both Luke and Cyprus's turn to freeze in place.

"You're afraid of horses?"

"Deathly." She scrunched her face and shut her eyes. "I've been imagining all of the many ways Cyprus was likely going to trample us to death the entire way here. I was on method number twenty-seven when he pulled that last little rearing stunt."

Though he fought it, a smile pulled at Luke's lips. "You think Cyprus is going to trample us? Jolene, he's a big teddy bear."

"That's not at all reassuring. I also have a deep-seated fear of bears."

"Well, that's actually not a bad fear to have. Bears can eat you. But I promise in all of my days, I've yet to meet a man-eating horse. They're entirely vegetarians. Just a bunch of hay eating, harmless herbivores."

"I want to tell you that your reasoning has completely dissolved a lifetime's worth of phobia, but sadly, I'm still just as scared and still just as anxious to get him put up for the night so we can get the heck outta Dodge."

Smirking, Luke pinned her with a stare. "Oh Jolene, that's not going to happen. We're going to conquer this fear of yours tonight. You've heard of immersion therapy before, haven't you?"

"You are *not* locking me and that animal in the barn alone."

"You're right, I'm not." Luke chuckled. "But I do want you to spend time with him. Sometimes our fears really aren't what we think they are. Sometimes they are something else entirely."

"Pretty sure I'm deathly afraid of *him*." Jolene's index finger jutted out to point at Cyprus.

"Please, just trust me." There was an imploring tone in his voice and a look in his eye.

Jolene assessed him for a labored pause, arms folded across her chest in unabashed defiance. Then, a sudden shift fell over her demeanor and she relented, "I trust you. Let's see what kind of magic you can work on this crazy fear of mine."

"Hey, you *are* the one who said Merrylark was full of it."

"I did," Jolene spoke through a smile. "And I believe it."

"Then I do, too."

13

JOLENE

ADMITTING HER FEAR to Luke wasn't as bad as she'd anticipated. If anything, she noticed how careful he became when guiding the horse around her, how he would take a purposefully wide berth, making certain there was no way a misstep could end in a smashed toe or foot. She could see how he'd slowed his motions, almost to show Jolene that Cyprus was capable of reciprocating the same calm and gentle movements he demonstrated.

For the first time, Jolene was in awe of the great creature. Luke choreographed a dance between the two. It was almost beautiful. *Almost.*

"Hand me a hoof pick?" Luke crouched down on the pine shaving floor, his legs tucked underneath him. "Should be right in that grooming bag."

"Can you describe what it is I'm looking for, exactly?" Fumbling through brushes and combs, Jolene pushed the items out of the way.

"It looks like something you'd pick a hoof with," he replied with a chuckle. Jolene noticed a wayward lock of hair that had fallen into Luke's eyes, and when he tossed his head to shake it off his brow, her heart caught on a beat. He was undeniably handsome when in his own element.

"Well, since I'd never *willingly* pick a hoof, I'm not sure what that sort of thing would look like."

"It looks like a tool."

That lock swept across his forehead again as he stayed hunched down on the floor, assessing Cyprus's hoof in question. Jolene found herself staring. She peered into the grooming bag again and pulled out the only thing resembling a pick: a small, handheld metal thing with a curved hook at the top. "This?"

"Bingo." Luke's hand reached out for it. "Thank you kindly."

"Sure." She gave him the pick and then darted back to her safe spot along the wall just outside of the stall. Her spine pressed against the plywood and she inhaled deeply through her nose. Even though she disliked horses, their smell wasn't off-putting. There was an earthy aroma of freshly cut fields of hay and grasses. Plus, Cyprus's stall was pristine. She'd expected manure or the stench of ammonia but this animal had clearly been well cared for. Loved, even.

"Well, I'll be." Luke pressed his palms to his knees and grunted softly as he stood up. "Found the reason for that awful limp."

"You did?" The lift in Jolene's tone was audible. She scurried toward him. "That quickly?"

"Abscess." Luke's strong fingers curled around the pick. "Nasty one, too. Let's see if we can locate some Epsom salt and a bucket for some hot water. We're going to have to soak that sucker."

"So we're not actually done here?" That hopeful tone took a crashing nosedive.

"Not quite yet." Pivoting, Luke faced Jolene. She tried to

keep her gaze from flitting up to that strand of hair that her fingers so itched to sweep out of his eyes.

"Ah, just what we need." Luke stretched up on his toes to retrieve a plastic tub from the top shelf of the tack room, directly over Jolene's head. She felt him invade her personal space and realized how welcome that invasion was. If she leaned just a step closer, they'd be touching. "This should be big enough for that enormous ol' hoof of his. Hold this for me?" He passed the bucket to her and scanned the shelves for salt. Stepping around her, Luke opened a cabinet located along the wall. Inside looked like a pharmacy—rows of prescriptions and bandages and gauze and wound dressing, all organized perfectly.

"That term 'healthy as a horse'?" He angled his head back toward Jolene. "It's a complete misnomer. All it takes is one misstep to end a racehorse's career and all it takes is a bad roll to end any horse's life. You know they've got right around seventy feet of intestine floating around in there? One kink and it's a life-saving surgery to the tune of ten grand."

"Ten thousand dollars?" Jolene was dumbfounded.

"Yes, ma'am."

Jolene really didn't need to know all of the details of equine veterinary care. Yet when she saw that spark in Luke's eye, the one brighter than any strand on her Christmas tree, she found herself wanting to enroll in every animal science course down at the local community college. She wanted to become an expert in the things Luke cared about.

The last time she felt this way about anyone was with Mark. Her fiancé had been an avid rock climber, and prior to meeting him, Jolene would've never thought of scaling a mountainside cliff just for the fun of it. But Mark made it seem so enticing. The stories he would tell from his days as a Boy Scout were the stuff of epic adventure novels. Jolene had wanted to experience that with him—to see life through his nature-loving lens. She wanted that rush of clinging on for dear life by only her fingertips, trusting her hands to find that next stronghold even if she couldn't see it.

She'd gone on a few of Mark's expeditions back when they'd first started dating. She visited a local outfitter and had just the right attire and all the gear necessary to ascend the highest mountain peak. She loved being with Mark, living out his passions.

Longer into their relationship, the treks up the mountains decreased in frequency, but it wasn't because Jolene didn't want to embark on the adventures anymore. It was just that Mark's ambitions outgrew her ability. She couldn't keep up, and though she considered herself to be outdoorsy, the escapades he would plan and the hills he would crest intimidated her. And they should have. She only wished they would've intimidated him a little, too. Maybe then this date on the calendar wouldn't be one plagued with such sadness and loss.

"Penny for your thoughts?" Luke lowered his gaze to search out Jolene's eyes. Jolene shook from her daydream and unfolded her arms wound tightly across her chest, like she could hold her memories in with physical force. She didn't want to tell Luke how often her thoughts drifted back to a snowy December day when her front door closed for the very last time behind the man she'd pledged her life to just the month before. When that last "I love you" was uttered and reciprocated. There wasn't supposed to be a finality in those three words. Love was an infinite and limitless thing.

"Jolene? You alright?" Gently, Luke bracketed her with

two hands on her biceps. She felt his fingers tighten on her arms, a slight squeeze of concern.

"I'm sorry, Luke. Sometimes I get a little lost up in this crazy head of mine."

Blue eyes burrowing into hers, he held her in a stare. "What I wouldn't give to get lost up there with you."

"You don't want to be inside my head, Luke. It's a mess."

"Actually I do."

Luke's words gave Jolene pause.

"You really want to know the thoughts I get lost in?" she asked. She wasn't sure if she wanted the statement to be a rhetorical one. And she wasn't sure how Luke perceived it. But she said it, needing the reassurance that everything would be okay if she did let him in through this small crack in her composure. If she shared these memories that looped in her mind like a long distance Olympic athlete racing around the track—that same, monotonous circle, over and over—would he want to pass the baton? Would he want to leave her to finish the race all on her own?

She breathed out forcefully through her mouth.

"I'm thinking about Decembers and good-byes that never had the chance to be spoken. I'm thinking about how horses scare me, but I've been afraid of other things before and I overcame those fears. I'm thinking about how I want to know more about you, but I'm scared to know more because you're leaving and I've been left before." She gulped past the large knot wedged in her throat. "I'm scared to feel alone again, because I've been alone for a long time now, and it's always harder to be alone right after someone disappears. I've learned there's a difference in degrees of loneliness, and I'd become comfortable with the kind I had for so many years. But I'm not sure I'm ready for a new lonely, and I'm worried that's what I'll feel when you leave Merrylark."

She stopped the words, putting the brakes on her confession. If Cyprus hadn't already proven to be lame, Jolene was sure Luke would've saddled him up and galloped as far away from her as he possibly could. That admission was enough to send any man running for the hills.

"Can you put the bucket down?" was all Luke responded.

Though she was unsure of the reason, she did so, settling the bucket by her feet.

Luke took a cautious step toward her. "Sometimes there are words to say in response and sometimes there are only actions. My words are failing me now. So all I know to do is just hold you, if that's alright by you."

It was alright. Completely. She nodded and pressed closer in.

Then, with the gentlest touch, Luke swept her up and curled her into his arms and even though she'd been there earlier that morning, it felt new in the best way possible. Her arms were idle at her sides as he held her. He held *onto* her, different from a hug or an embrace which never lasted quite long enough.

She felt his cheek against her hair, felt him inhale softly, a warm breath feathering on her skin. She felt his firm chest through the fabric of his jacket. She felt his strong fingers run up and down her back, like he was tenderly plucking on the strings of a guitar. When she pulled her arms from her sides and slid them around his waist, she felt him lean in even closer, their bodies bundled together in the frigid, drafty old barn.

She felt all of those things, but most notably, she felt protected. A blizzard could sweep through that very stall and she knew, without a doubt, she'd be safe if she stayed here, bracketed in Luke's arms.

"I'm scared, too, Jolene," he whispered into her hair.

"You are?" She angled her head up to look at him without pulling out from his grasp.

"Of course. I'm scared of the future. Of being alone. I haven't told you yet, but this week—here in Merrylark—this was supposed to be my honeymoon week."

Jolene had figured as much since the original lake house reservation was made for two, but she was grateful for the information, mostly because it meant Luke was comfortable opening up to her, too. It felt good to have that vulnerability reciprocated.

"My ex-fiancé had a slight change of plans when it came to getting married. Well, getting married to me, at least." Luke made a huffing noise that sounded like a chuckle, but one of disbelief rather than true laughter. "That's how I wound up here in Merrylark, all by lonesome at the lake house. But you know what?"

"What's that?"

"I feel anything but alone. From you and your incredible hospitality to my new friends Roger and Millie to your sister and her family to Devon—I feel more a part of something than I've ever felt in my life. I'm surrounded by people who care and even though I don't know what my future holds, I really like my present."

Jolene snuggled in closer, resting her head against Luke's jacket pocket. "I like my present, too."

"Even with that terrifying horse just a few feet away?"

"Especially with that terrifying horse. I have to face the fact that without Cyprus and his sudden lameness, I wouldn't have this time with you right now. And I'm really enjoying this time with you, Luke. A lot."

Luke's smile deepened. "I'm pretty sure I can arrange for

more if you'd like it." He paused, as if in thought. "Yep. Just checked my calendar and it's wide open for the rest of the week."

Jolene laughed.

"In fact, I'd happily clear out any amount of time you'd be willing to spend with me, Jolene."

"How about dinner tomorrow night?" She couldn't believe it. Cat had challenged her to ask Luke out, but it wasn't something she ever thought she'd do. But here she was, standing in a barn asking this man to join her for dinner the next evening. If he hadn't been holding her firmly in his arms, she would've attempted to dig herself a hole and crawl into it.

"Did you just ask me out on a date?"

Jolene buried her head in his jacket, hoping to disappear. "I think so," she groaned.

Luke pushed her out at arm's length. "That's not exactly how things go where I come from. Can't say I'm not flattered, but let's do this a different way." With his thumb and index finger, he touched her chin and angled her head so he could look directly into her eyes. "Jolene Carter, would you by any chance care to join me for dinner tomorrow night?"

Jolene's stomach somersaulted. "Absolutely."

"How 'bout lunch?"

"Of course."

"Want to grab breakfast somewhere while we're at it, too?"

Laughing and regaining just bit of her composure, she answered, "Definitely."

"What do you say we just spend the entire day together? Think that will work with your schedule?"

"Nothing could make me happier."

Bringing her into his chest in a bear hug, Luke said, "Looks like Gary and Martha did a pretty bang up job of channeling their inner Santa Claus magic, because I just got my wish."

Even though she hadn't wished it out loud, Jolene had gotten hers, too.

14

LUKE

THREE KNOCKS RATTLED the metal screen door. Luke had been dead to the world, all cozied up under flannels sheets and the thickest patchwork quilt he'd ever touched. He heard two more knocks. That was enough to convince Luke that his alarm for the morning would be in the form of an assertive fist on the lake house front door. Not a whole lot better than the blaring beep of his truck being towed just the day before.

Sitting up, he reached for the discarded white t-shirt slung over the back of the wicker chair near the bed. He tugged it over his torso and pulled tight on the drawstring to his flannel pajama pants. Rubbing his fists in his eye sockets, he stumbled out of the bedroom, down the hall, and toward the front door that jostled again with a booming thud.

"Coming!" Luke hollered, his tired voice cracking on the syllables.

Luke pulled on the door handle. Crisp dawn light blasted through the open frame, a halo of gold shining around Patrick, Jolene's brother-in-law. "Morning, neighbor." The cheery voice did not at all match the determined knocking from just moments before. "I wake you?"

Luke held in the comment that Patrick likely woke all of Merrylark with his knocking. He just nodded and grinned.

"Sorry for that. Listen, you have a minute to chat? Mind if I come in?" Patrick stepped over the threshold without waiting on an answer.

Luke backed up. "I'd offer you a cup of coffee, but I still haven't made it to the store."

"That's fine. I've already had some." Patrick surveyed the lake house in a big sweeping gaze which ultimately fell upon the decorated tree placed in the middle of the room. "Would you look at that? Jolene wasn't kidding. That tree looks fantastic!"

"Thank you, but all the credit goes directly to her. I had very little to do with it."

"She sure does love Christmas, doesn't she?"

Luke nodded again, covering his mouth when a yawn replaced his tired grin.

"Again, sorry to wake you. There's just something I needed to talk with you about before Rose and I head back home. Since the van's all packed and the girls are waiting on me to go, I figured I couldn't put it off any longer."

Patrick shifted from one foot to the other. His vacillating movements made Luke wary.

"I have the sneaking suspicion you didn't come over here to talk Christmas décor." Luke tried to manufacture his most jovial tone and matching expression. It was hard to do at this early hour. "There another reason for your unexpected drop in?"

With a determined stride forward, Patrick pressed close to Luke. Then, taking Luke completely off-guard, Patrick thrust his index finger into Luke's chest and breathed hotly through his mouth.

"If you ever do anything to hurt Jolene, I will see to it that you never set foot not only in Merrylark ever again, but in this entire county. In fact, make that the whole dang state!"

Bewildered, Luke thought for a moment he might be dreaming—that this act of intimidation was a continuation of some bizarre dream. But the finger poking his chest was enough to make him realize that the encounter was, in fact, happening, odd as that was.

"Patrick, I promise you, I have absolutely no intention of hurting Jolene. None whatsoever."

"Of course you don't *intend* to." Patrick pulled his finger back, but curled it into a fist. He pulsed his fingers open and closed. Suddenly, his shoulders slouched and all pretense vanished. "Listen Luke, I absolutely hate confrontation. This right here?" He fluttered his hands between them. "This is just me trying to be the protective brother-in-law. It's my job to make sure Jolene doesn't get her heart broken. Again. Because even though you two have only known each other for a few short days, I can say without a doubt that you've already got a piece of her heart, whether you've asked for it or not. I need you to know that, because now it's your responsibility to make sure you take care of it." His chest puffed up. "And I'm not leaving here until I have your word that you won't hurt that woman, because if you do—"

"I will not hurt Jolene," Luke interjected. "I know it might sound crazy, but she's got a piece of my heart, too. And to be completely frank with you, before coming here, I didn't even think I had any pieces left to offer anyone."

The two men looked at one another, not to size the other up, but in mutual understanding.

"You're a good brother, Patrick." Luke clamped a hand on his shoulder. "But as a lawyer, I sure thought you'd have a little more finesse when trying to intimidate."

"That's the thing—I don't need to intimidate anyone when I'm in the courtroom. I've got facts and knowledge on my side. That's what makes me so uneasy about this whole deal with you and Jolene. I don't have *any* facts when it comes to you. I hardly know anything about you. And neither does Jolene. No offense, but you're just some cowboy stranger who strode into town and swept her off her feet. So forgive me for coming across strong—or for trying to, at least. I'm just not willing to take any risks when it comes to Jolene's happiness. Lord knows she finally deserves a little."

Luke let those words sink in once Patrick left. Jolene did deserve happiness, but was he the one to give it to her? Was it selfish to want to spend more time with her, knowing all the while that he'd be back in his truck in just a few days, heading home to the ranch to pick life up where he left it? After spending the entire day with her like they'd planned, would it be as easy to end things once his week at the lake house came to a close?

Who was he kidding? Luke knew a day with Jolene would only make their inevitable goodbye that much more difficult. Maybe it made sense to cut ties now, while things were still new and fresh. He thought about calling it all off when the vibration of his phone scooting across the kitchen counter interrupted his thoughts. He picked it up and swiped across the screen.

"Hello?"

"Luke?"

"Yes sir," Luke replied.

"Good morning, Luke. It's Thomas Riley, from Silent Night Stables."

"Mornin', Thomas. How are things going today for our boy Cyprus? He was in a bad way last night, poor old horse."

"Well, Luke, that's the reason I'm calling. He's not really looking any better. In fact, my untrained eye tells me he might even be worse. Hobbling around and not putting any weight on that foot. I've never seen him so uncomfortable."

"That abscess might be 'bout ready to burst," Luke said. "Mind if I come over and take a look at it?"

"Ah, would you? I hate to ask, especially after all the time you spent here last night, but I fear I'm no good to him."

"It's no problem at all, Thomas. Happy to help. I'll be over within the hour."

❄

LUKE ALWAYS KNEW the path he'd take in life would be the same, worn out ruts on the road his father and grandfather paved years before. His destination was always to take over the ranch. One day it would be his, and the mustangs and the hayfields and the barn and all the income that generated would fill his bank account, just like it had his parents' when his grandfather passed away and they were left with the inheritance.

It always sounded like a good plan—a solid one. One that stood the test of time, and in this day with a wavering economy and unpredictable employment options, the ranch was a sure, tried and true bet. Luke never thought to dream of anything different for his life.

But Merrylark had him dreaming.

❄

"PASS ME THAT level when you get a chance?" Devon called over his shoulder as he balanced on the middle step of the ladder. "This trim doesn't look straight at all to me."

"Nah, your eyeballs are just crooked." Luke handed off the tool.

"Hey, not all of us are blessed with such perfectly symmetrical, handsome faces like yours, Handley."

Luke chuckled. "This old mug?" He waved a palm over his face. "Hardly symmetrical and definitely not handsome."

"I know of at least one Merrylark maiden who would beg to differ." Devon nodded toward the huge picture window facing Glenn Street. "Speaking of, isn't that her walking up the street right now?"

Luke rolled his wrist over to look at his watch. It was just approaching noon and, as promised, Jolene was about to show up at Devon's renovation project. Luke had needed to postpone their breakfast in order to tend to Cyprus, but that had been okay with him. Instead of three meals together, they'd only share two. One-third less opportunity to keep from falling for her. That's what he tried to tell himself but he knew it was nonsense. He was all in.

"I'd be lying if I said I wasn't jealous, Luke. I mean, not necessarily of your face, but of the fact that you've somehow managed to gain the affection of one of the most genuine, kindhearted women I've ever had the privilege of knowing." Devon stepped down from the ladder and walked toward his friend. "After Mark, I never thought I'd ever see her this happy again. I think you have a lot to do with that."

"But I'm leaving."

"Sure. You're *leaving*. Future tense. You haven't left yet, and I know it's none of my business, but I do have to say, you'd be a fool to actually *leave*. No one in their right mind would willingly leave a woman like Jolene," Devon said. "I know I sure wouldn't."

"It's not that easy, Devon. I have obligations back home. A ranch to tend to. Mom and Dad aren't exactly spring chickens, and let's face it, there's not much here for me to do with the very few skills I've been blessed with."

Devon crossed his arms over his upper body. "I think you grossly underestimate what an asset you are to a town like ours. Didn't you just act as a vet to Thomas's old horse this morning?" Luke gave a hesitant nod. "And I think you're also underestimating just how much a certain someone has fallen for you. You need to start seeing things for what they are."

At that instant, Jolene appeared in the open frame of the door, two brown lunch sacks in hand and a grin spread ear to ear.

"I've arrived with sustenance and sweets!" She jostled the bags in the air. "Made a quick stop down at The Rolling Pin. Hope you boys are hungry!"

"Famished." Devon collapsed to the floor to sit with his legs crisscrossed. "How was the bakery today?"

"As crowded as ever." Jolene passed off the bags and slid to sit on the hardwood next to Luke and Devon, avoiding the tools that littered the floor.

"I keep trying to get Aunt Martha to expand that shop. Believe it or not, I just happen to know a guy who will have a pretty spectacular storefront up for rent shortly. Can't convince her to sign the lease, though. Aunt Martha just doesn't think she needs that much space for a bakery."

"She could easily pack it out," Luke said as he pulled a ham and cheese sandwich out of a clear plastic bag. He bit into it and savored the homemade taste. It reminded him of the sandwiches his mother would pack in his lunchbox back when he was a kid. Simple, but full of love.

"I agree," Devon said. "But she says I should save it for a tenant who won't fold after the first month."

"There's no way The Rolling Pin would ever go under. I'm absolutely convinced Martha and Gary's baked goods are what keep this entire town running," Jolene said matter-of-factly. "Well, that and Cat's coffee. The only thing better than a maple iced scone is a maple iced scone with a cappuccino."

"Sounds like the two would make good business partners," Luke said absentmindedly as he polished off the last bite of sandwich.

"You're absolutely right about that, Luke." Jolene tilted her head in thought. "I know Cat has a love-hate relationship with that food truck. She originally wanted to open up a storefront, but as Devon can attest to, prime real estate in this town doesn't come up all too often."

"The very reason my dad and I snatched this place up as soon as it became available."

"Sounds like that might be something worth exploring," Luke noted. "Cat's Rolling Coffee Pin."

Jolene giggled and covered her mouth. "Not sure a place with that name would be a huge hit." Her shoulders bounced up and down with laughter.

"Cup of Coffee and Some Baked Stuff," Devon deadpanned.

"While I appreciate the straightforwardness of it, maybe something a little less wordy?"

"Cup of Joe?" Luke suggested.

Jolene's eyes lit up. "I love it! Now that's a place I would visit every day, and not just because my name is in the title. And speaking of prime real estate, I have to cut our lunch visit short. The O'Connells called this morning and they're actually thinking of putting the lake house on the market after all these years. I've got to run back to meet the realtor by one o'clock." She packed up the empty bags and wrappers left over from their lunch. "But let's pick this conversation back up later. I think we might really be onto something."

"Care to chat over dinner?" Luke already knew they had plans to spend the evening together, but he just couldn't resist asking her out again. It felt so good to do so.

"Absolutely. Six o'clock?"

"On the dot."

15
—

JOLENE

EVEN THOUGH GLENN Street was just a few short miles from home, the Christmas season congestion impacted their small town, clogging the roadways with holiday shoppers and errand runners. Jolene kept glancing at the clock on her dash, wishing not to keep the realtor waiting. She'd been stopped at the one light in town for nearly five minutes, and a deer and her babies held her up on the two lane highway. Evidently they weren't in as much of a rush as she, as they pranced along the snow-slicked road like they belonged hitched to Santa's sleigh.

By the time Jolene's tires turned into her driveway, she could see the realtor standing outside the lake house, anticipating Jolene's arrival with a large leather bag over her shoulder and a scowl on her face.

"I'll be right there!" Jolene hollered, racing up the steps to her home. "Just have to let the dog out real quick!"

She fit the key into the bolt and jogged to the back room where Ace lay sleeping on the queen-sized bed.

"Okay, buddy. Go do your business. *Quickly.*" She held the back door open for him, tapping her foot while he took care of things. When he bounded back into the house, she planted a kiss on his head and gave him a quick scratch behind his ears. "I'll take you on that walk as soon as I'm done with this meeting. Promise."

Pulling the door shut behind her, Jolene hurried toward the neighboring home, feeling frazzled and unkempt, the exact opposite of the gorgeous, yet stern, woman who stood on the *Welcome* mat of the O'Connell house. She was tall and slender with cheekbones that belonged in a beauty marketing campaign. Her dark hair hung sleek and straight to the middle of her back, and even the way she swept it over her shoulder was both lovely and intimidating.

"I'm so sorry!" Jolene stammered as she sprinted up to the house. Her hands worked to open the front door. "Got held up in town and then traffic was an absolute bear. Actually, a deer, but that's a different story." Something about the woman's commanding presence made Jolene nervous. "Did you run into any traffic on the way up here? Road 29 tends to be a bit less clogged this time of year. Unless you cut over and took 42. That's a road you wouldn't want to be caught on the second week of December. Without fail, you'll get stuck behind one of those massive snow plows and then you might as well call off any plans for the day. Those things move slower than snails." Jolene had no control over the babbling. "So...this is the place. Feel free to take a look around and let me know if I can answer any questions for you. I live just next door and if I can be completely honest here, I probably know this place better than the owners do. Just holler if you need me."

Before the woman could open her mouth to respond, Jolene had left, anxious to create some distance between them and eager to focus on her much anticipated dinner date with Luke later that evening.

❄

THERE WAS ONE nice restaurant in Merrylark: Shanley's. On Thursdays, they served a prime rib dinner, and as though Jolene's stomach could predict the day of the week, she'd been craving the delicious meal all day long. To pass the time, she'd gone out for an afternoon run with Ace. Running had a miraculous way of clearing Jolene's head. She could focus on the crunching of ice under her tennis shoes and suddenly all of her worries slipped out of her tense shoulders and her jumbled mind, like she could stomp her stresses out through her feet.

On her final stretch home, she caught sight of Hank's tow truck lumbering up the road ahead.

"Hey there, cousin," Hank hollered out the rolled down window as Jolene jogged up in the bike lane next to him. "Got your friend's truck all tuned up and running again. Easy fix. Mind if I park it in your driveway? Looks like his is occupied."

Jolene noticed the realtor's BMW still parked outside the lake house. She frowned. "That's strange." She shook her head. "Of course, feel free to leave it just behind mine. Let me know what the bill is and I'll get it paid."

"Free of charge. Friends and family discount."

"A discount of one-hundred percent? That's one mighty big discount, Hank."

"'Tis the season." Hank tipped his hat and revved the engine. "I'll get this truck unloaded and be out of your hair. Happy holidays, cousin."

"Same to you, Hank."

❄

LUKE CALLED AROUND 4:00 to ask if it would be alright if the two met at the restaurant instead of their original plan to have Luke pick Jolene up at her house. He'd been held up at Devon's putting the finishing touches on the studio space. Though he said he was embarrassed to start their date off in separate cars, Jolene didn't mind at all. In fact, she was excited about the surprise she'd been cooking up all afternoon and couldn't wait to see the look on Luke's face when she pulled up to Shanley's.

At 6:00 p.m. when Jolene angled Luke's precious Bessie into an open spot directly in front of the restaurant's entrance doors, she instantly noticed Luke's dropped jaw and wide, unbelieving eyes.

"Doesn't she look great?" Jolene said as she stepped out of the driver's seat and onto the curb, careful to balance on the pointed heels she had precious little practice walking on.

"She's breathtaking," Luke uttered. "The most beautiful thing I've ever laid eyes on."

Jolene's breath caught when he leaned in to brush a light kiss on her cheek.

Luke took hold of her hand and stepped back to admire his date for the evening. For Jolene, comfort was usually the determining factor when making a wardrobe selection, but tonight she'd intentionally changed her ways. She wanted to dress up for Luke. She wanted to be beautiful for him. After trying on nearly every dress in her closet, she decided on a black number with an empire waist and sequined bodice and long bell sleeves. It had been an impulse buy years back when she'd first eyed it in a local dress shop window. She'd walked passed that dress over a dozen times before returning to the store and forking over way too much for it. Since that moment, she'd often regretted that rash decision, the thick layer of dust that covered the garment bag a reminder that she'd never have the occasion nor the person worthy of that magical dress.

But then she met Luke and suddenly it felt like she could wear the dress every day of her life.

"You look so incredibly beautiful, Jolene."

Tucking her chin, she looked down at her feet. "Did you see Bessie?" She stepped to the side. "She's up and running again, compliments of Hank. Quite literally—all of the work he did was completely complimentary, free of charge."

"Hardly even noticed her." Luke leaned in to sweep another kiss on her cheek and this time he lingered for just long enough that Jolene could smell his cologne. "You in that amazing dress kind of eclipses everything else. But you must be freezing." He ran both hands up and down her arms. "Let's get inside. Our table should be ready for us."

Jolene followed Luke into Shanley's, taking the time to appreciate just how nice he looked, too. He wore a black and red plaid flannel shirt which looked suspiciously like something out of Devon's closet. But Devon never looked anywhere close to as handsome as Luke did with it tucked into dark denim jeans. His black cowboy boots were the perfect finishing touch. Jolene found herself smiling—giddy almost—over the fact that she was on a date with the most handsome man in the room. Make that, the most handsome man in Merrylark.

Once inside, the hostess guided them toward their table. It was the best one in the house, tucked cozily into the far corner, right next to a stone fireplace that was draped with holiday garlands and strung with silver sparkling tinsel. Tall red and white pillar candles twisted like candy canes flickered on the mantle and wrapped packages were stacked neatly on the hearth as if they were under a tree. Stockings with what Jolene recognized as the names of the wait staff hung among the festive décor. It was a beautiful sight.

"Your table." The hostess held out her hand.

Luke scurried to slide out Jolene's chair, handing her the black folded napkin to lay across her lap after she took her seat.

"Thank you," she said, blushing when he pushed her chair back in and sat down across from her, his eyes never faltering from hers.

"Eric, your waiter, will be right with you."

The young hostess left the two alone, and though Jolene had been alone with Luke on multiple occasions over the last few days, in this moment, she felt truly anxious to be in his presence. This wasn't the casual cup of coffee they'd shared the first day they'd met. This was a formal, sit down meal, and Jolene couldn't bring to mind the last time she'd had a proper date like this. She felt out of practice and out of her element.

Releasing their locked gaze for just a moment, Luke let out an audible breath. "Whew," he uttered as his shoulders dropped. "I'm *really* nervous."

"Me too!" Jolene half shouted. Luke eyes bulged at the volume of her reply and they both burst into laughter. Reaching across the table, he covered her hand with his.

"I'm so sorry I couldn't pick you up. But I have to admit, watching you step out of my truck in that dress was just about the best thing I've ever seen."

Though she hadn't known it earlier, that was the exact reaction her heart had been hoping to hear.

"You said Hank isn't going to charge anything for the work he did?"

"He just said 'happy holidays' and that it was on him. Friends and family discount."

Luke grinned, but Jolene could tell that didn't sit well with him. "I just don't feel right about letting him do all that work without any sort of pay."

"Didn't you pay several hundred dollars to have her towed?" Jolene asked. Luke nodded. "I'd just consider that as a prepayment for the labor he ultimately did on the truck."

"I suppose I could try to look at it that way."

Just then, their waiter walked up to their table. Jolene had been waited on by him before and knew him to be the son of the town's mayor. He was young—just out of high school—with floppy dark hair and a large, toothy smile that seemed too big for his face.

"Hi there," he said, bouncing on the balls of his feet. "Welcome to Shanley's. My name's Eric and I'll be waiting on you two this evening. As you might already know, tonight's a set menu of prime rib and garlic mashed pota-toes. A Caesar salad will begin the meal, and we'll finish up with a flourless chocolate cake. Would you like to start off with anything to drink besides water?"

"Maybe a bottle of your house merlot?"

"Of course." Eric bowed a little. "I'll bring that right out, along with some bread and butter."

Jolene remembered Luke had said he didn't often drink, so she was surprised by his order.

"Up for bit of wine tasting tonight?" she said, smiling after Eric left. "I thought you said you didn't really drink much."

"I don't," Luke admitted. "I just figured that's what you were supposed to do on a date. I can't tell you how long it's been since I've been on a first date, Jolene. I'm trying to remember what it looks like from the movies I've seen."

That made Jolene laugh. "You're doing just fine, Luke.

Just be yourself. That's the person I've started falling—" She halted. Luke's eyes filled with intrigue, awaiting her words. "Falling for."

Luke squeezed her hand, then let go as a basket of bread was delivered to their table, placed in between them. "How did the meeting with the realtor go?"

"It didn't."

"No? How come?" Luke took out a roll and began to butter it with his knife.

"It was a bit of a whirlwind. I had to let the dog out and the realtor had clearly been waiting for me to arrive for a while and I don't know...there was just something overly intimidating about her. I can't put my finger on it."

"I find it hard to believe you could ever be intimidated by any woman. Seems like it should be the other way around."

"She was stunning, Luke. Like one of those women who belonged on a magazine spread. All polished and gorgeous."

"Like the one sitting across from me right now?"

Jolene took a bite of bread and laughed. "A line from another movie?"

"Nope, that's a genuine Luke Handley quote right there."

She liked flirting with Luke, and they continued these little back and forth exchanges all the way until their main course arrived. When the two heaping plates of meat and potatoes were settled in front of them, Jolene rubbed her stomach in appreciation, the smell both mouthwatering and delectable. She might've even smacked her lips, but if she did, that was completely unintentional.

"This looks and smells amazing." She picked up her knife and fork, ready to dig in.

"Sure does." Luke reached out for her hand. "Mind if I say grace for us first?"

Jolene set her utensils back down and took Luke's hand in hers, bowing her head as he gave thanks for their meal and their friendship. As Luke prayed over their meal, everything felt right, calm and just as it should be.

Fluttering her eyes open, Jolene glanced across the table, so grateful for the man opposite her, and so thankful for his kind and thoughtful heart. She knew her look reflected that appreciation so she felt a sudden, hollow and bottoming-out sensation in her stomach when she saw the exact opposite reflected in Luke's eyes.

16

LUKE

LUKE HAD TO BLINK multiple times just to be sure he wasn't seeing things. Sometimes his mind did that —played tricks on him at the most inopportune times. It happened once as a teenager back on the ranch. He'd just finished work and was heading back to the barn to put his gelding in the stall when he swore he saw a lone mare up on the ridge, separated from the rest of the herd. He'd squinted and strained, but couldn't make out that it was just a craggily old boulder until he was nearly on top of it. He always figured he probably needed glasses, and this moment in the restaurant only solidified that inkling.

"Luke?" Jolene dipped her chin to search out his eyes. "You okay?"

A sudden chiming came from under the table, the digital sound of bells jingling. Jolene ducked down and scooped up her black leather purse. "Phone. Sorry." She looked at the screen. "Oh! It's the realtor. I should probably take this. Excuse me for a moment?" She covered the mouthpiece and pushed back from the table. "I'll just be a second. Hello? Yes, this is Jolene."

Luke's breath hissed out between his lips as soon as Jolene was out of earshot. Everything in his body felt tense, like a rubber band stretched to capacity. There was an uneasy feeling churning in his gut and he clamped his eyes shut, hoping when he opened them, the scene before him would be a different one.

That particular Christmas wish was not granted.

Kiara's eyes met his from across the room.

"Luke," he could see her mouth just above the rim of a martini glass held to her lips. She smiled at him like she hadn't been the one to break his heart just six months ago.

Kiara set her glass down, rose to her feet and slid out from behind the bar, making her way across the room with measured strides.

"Luke," she said again when he stood from his seat in greeting, as he was accustomed to do whenever a lady came to into the room. She wrapped her arms around his neck and placed a kiss on his cheek.

Luke drew back instantly.

"Kiara? What are you doing here?" He put his hands on her waist to push her back, creating distance between them. "In Merrylark?"

Her smile fell from her lips and eyes. "We've had this on the calendar for almost a year, Luke."

There was no logic in her statement. Luke grit his teeth. "So was our wedding, but that didn't stop you from changing those plans."

"Luke," she said again, her tone pleading. She always said his name like it was the preface to a question. "Luke, we need to talk."

"Not right now." He sat back down at the table and placed his napkin on his lap.

Kiara followed suit and slid into Jolene's chair.

"That seat's already taken."

Her lips pressed together tightly. She stood to collect a chair from the empty table next to them and then lowered into it. "Luke, I'm sorry."

Luke tore into the prime rib, sawing it with his knife. He shoved a huge bite into his mouth. It was delicious but he had trouble enjoying it.

"Luke, will you listen to me?" Kiara's hand reached across the table to touch his arm. Luke recoiled, his eyes widening. "Luke, please."

"Can't you see I'm busy, Kiara? I'm here..." He lowered his voice. "On a date."

For a split second, Luke felt guilt over the brief display of hurt that flitted over Kiara's face. While he'd been irreparably hurt by Kiara's decision to call off their wedding, he didn't want to hurt her. He'd lived enough life to know that an eye for an eye just left everyone blind, unable to see things for what they really were.

"We can talk," he relented. "But it'll have to be later. This night is supposed to be a special one and having my ex-fiancé show up was not in the original plans."

"Thank you, Luke. So much." Kiara wrapped her hands over Luke's once more. He hated the way it reminded him of the years they'd spent together and a time in their relationship when a gesture of this sort brought him joy. All it made him want to do now was wash his hands, like he could wash away their past. "We can chat when you get back to the house. I'll be sure to wait up."

"Wait." His eyes flashed. "You're staying at the lake house?"

"The neighbor woman let me in this afternoon. Don't worry, I'm planning to sleep on the couch, but I'll have to find a few extra blankets to keep warm. That pellet stove doesn't seem like it'll be enough to heat the entire place—"

"We both can't stay at the lake house, Kiara."

She smirked like he'd said something foolish. "Luke, it'll be fine. It *is* supposed to be our honeymoon week."

He set his glass on the table harder than he'd intended. Water sloshed over the rim onto the white tablecloth. "Please stop saying that, Kiara. I know what week it is."

"I'll see you back at the house. We'll talk things over. Enjoy your dinner, Luke. It's really good to see you again. Really good."

With that Kiara stood from her borrowed chair and retraced her steps through the restaurant, brushing shoulders with Jolene whose eyes were fixed on her phone as she scurried over to their table.

"Sorry!" Jolene said when she returned, obviously flustered. "That was so strange. It was the realtor apologizing for not making it by the house this afternoon. Said her daughter came down with a terrible case of the stomach flu and that she'd have to reschedule for sometime next week." Jolene kept staring at her phone like she could find the answers written on the screen. "But I swear I let her in. I let someone in, at least." Her eyes rounded. "Oh gosh, Luke! What if I let a robber into the lake house?"

"You didn't let a robber in, Jolene."

"But I let *someone* in. Someone who looked like a woman with a purpose. She had a big bag and seemed like she was really supposed to be there."

"That's because she *was* supposed to be there."

Jolene's face took on a puzzled expression.

"It was Kiara. My ex-fiancé."

"Oh." All color drained from Jolene's cheeks and her body slumped in her chair. "I see."

"No, you don't because I don't even see, to be truthful. All I know is that Kiara is in Merrylark and wants to talk to me about something. She was just here." He glanced to the extra chair at their table like it was an elephant in the room. Jolene traced the path of his eyes, understanding. "I don't know what she could possibly want to talk about, Jolene. Everything between us was settled long ago. Over and done with."

"Luke, you don't have to explain anything to me. It's okay. I'll be sure to give you two your space—"

"There is no 'us two.' I'm serious when I say I have no feelings left for Kiara. In fact, seeing her here tonight only made me realize just how wrong we were for each other. It feels like another life altogether; one I don't want to relive any time soon."

A trace of a smile lifted the corner of Jolene's mouth.

"I don't want to think about her anymore this evening." With his foot, he pushed the unwelcome chair away from their table. "I just want to enjoy this delicious meal and the incredible company."

"I think I can arrange that." Cutting a forkful from her prime rib, she lifted it into the air as a salute. "To the best steak dinner in Merrylark!" Luke raised his fork and clinked it against Jolene's. "In fairness, it's the only steak dinner even offered in Merrylark, but it still feels worthy of toasting." She lowered her fork to her plate, a contemplative look on her face. "Luke, I'm sorry for the things I said earlier about Kiara, back when I thought she was the realtor. I shouldn't have judged her so quickly and even though you're not together now, you obviously cared for her at one point, and for her to be worthy of that, she must be a good person."

Luke chuckled. "You give my teenage hormones too much credit."

"You've known her since you were a teenager?" Jolene gaped. "I didn't realize your history together was so long."

Sighing, Luke said, "That's exactly what it is, though. History. Not the present. Speaking of which, I got *you* a little present today." Reaching down, Luke pulled out a small, red box adorned with a glittering gold bow. He placed it on the table between them.

"That was the best segue I've ever heard, Luke. Super impressive."

"I'm trying really hard over here. Gotta give a guy some credit." He slid the box closer to her. "Go ahead. Open it."

Taking the delicately wrapped package in her hands, Jolene slid off the bow and opened the lid. "Well, this one I can definitely handle!" Hooking it over her finger, Jolene lifted a small ornament of a Clydesdale from the box. "If only they came in this size in real life!"

"There is actually such a thing as a miniature horse, you know. Totally different than a pony."

"No kidding?"

"Yep." Luke tipped his head. "Just a shrunken down version of the big horses, but most of the time triple the attitude. Little man complex or something. We've got a mini pinto back at the ranch named Gus Gus. He thinks he runs the place, little devil."

"I'd sure love to meet him sometime."

The hope of taking Jolene home someday to meet his family and see his ranch was one Luke could latch onto. But while he wanted more than anything to make future plans, he had a past waiting for him back at the lake house that he needed to deal with first.

17

JOLENE

THE WOMAN SHE thought was the realtor was actually Luke's ex-fiancé. That truth kept spinning in Jolene's head like a pirouetting Sugar Plum fairy. She couldn't keep from envisioning Kiara in a stunning white gown, her handsome groom waiting under an arbor of evergreen and sprigs of holly. She'd pictured poinsettia topiaries flanking the church pews, a path of white rose petals sprinkled up the aisle that led to Kiara's fairytale future.

It was a weird thing to do, to imagine the details of a wedding for the man she'd been on a date with just earlier that evening, but she just couldn't help it. Luke and Kiara were stunning together, like the ceramic bride and groom figurines that adorned the top tier of a wedding cake.

Jolene had a far easier time picturing Kiara and Luke together than she did placing herself in that wedding day scenario.

Her entire mood had shifted once back at her home. Their car ride from Shanley's was nice—quiet, but the kind of quiet that felt restful. And when Luke had taken Jolene's hand in his, she felt a swarm of butterflies take flight in her stomach. He'd stroked the back of her hand lightly with his thumb and though his hands were calloused and rough from ranch work, it was such a gentle gesture that Jolene felt it warm her entire body.

There was no question she was falling in love with this man. Pretend as she might, she knew without a doubt he held the keys to her heart. Unfortunately, she had a feeling she wasn't the only woman to make that assertion.

After cozying up in her reindeer-printed flannel pants and fuzzy red sweatshirt, Jolene warmed a cup of cocoa and snuggled onto the couch with Ace to begin a marathon of holiday romance movies. She loved that she could find a Christmas movie on all hours of the day or night beginning in mid-November. It always helped her get in the mood for the upcoming holiday. Tonight, however, sweet romances all tied in neat bows did little to offer any solace. They just reminded her of how unraveled everything suddenly felt now that Luke's ex was in Merrylark.

When the final credits for the first movie began rolling on the screen, Jolene walked to the kitchen to refill her mug. She grabbed a treat for Ace from the glass jar on the counter and, though she didn't mean to, her gaze drifted out the window and into that of the lake house next door. It was pitch black inside, apart from a few twinkling pillar candles placed sporadically within the home, glowing a warm golden light.

Jolene's heart sank.

"Sure didn't take any time to rekindle the romance," she said to Ace who came to her side the moment he heard the treat jar open. She dropped a doggie biscuit into his mouth and ruffled the thick fur on his head. "Looks like it's back to just the two of us, Ace."

Lifting his paw, he placed it on Jolene's slipper clad foot.

She dipped down and wrapped her arms around Ace, her constant companion throughout the last few years. That dog always knew when she needed a hug and Jolene swore he gave the best hugs around.

"Why did I let myself get so caught up in the idea of not being alone for the holidays for once?" she spoke into his fur. "At least I've always got you, buddy. We're a good team, right?"

Ace barked.

"That's right. Just you and me. BFF's forever." Barking again, Ace bolted for the front door. "Well that didn't last long, either. Thanks a lot." Jolene pushed up to stand. A knock on the door sent Ace into another barking fit, this time complete with tail chasing and spinning circles. "Okay boy. Scooch on over."

Jolene opened the door. On the other side of the threshold stood Kiara, her nose red and cheeks splotchy with cold.

"Hi. Jolene, is it? We met briefly this afternoon." She lifted her hand in a cordial wave. "I'm Kiara. I'm staying next door. I hate to bother you, but it looks like the power's gone out. It's like an ice box in there. Completely freezing."

"Oh goodness, I'm so sorry—"

"I'm assuming a refund will be issued for today's portion of the reservation, but even that won't magically make the place heat up. It's unlivable."

Taken aback at Kiara's assertive tone, Jolene was at a loss for words. Her tongue tied in her mouth.

"For the time being, I assume you can put me up in the nearest hotel? One *with* a working heater."

Ace sneered, making Jolene chuckle.

"I'm sorry." Kiara's brow tightened. "Is there something funny I'm missing?"

"Only that Merrylark doesn't have a hotel."

"An inn, then. Bed and breakfast."

"Don't have one of those either."

Eyes rolling, Kiara huffed an audible groan. "Fine. Just find me a suitable place to stay where I don't have to worry that I'll get hypothermia or frostbite in my sleep."

"The only place I can offer you is my spare guest room, but there's a good chance you'll be sharing it with this guy." Jolene pointed to Ace. "He likes to curl up on the quilt on cold nights. He's a terrific snuggler, though. You'll be thankful for the extra warmth."

"Well isn't this evening going just swimmingly?" Kiara muttered loud enough for Jolene to hear. She threw two hands into the air. "Fine. I suppose that will have to do. I'll be back over after I gather my things from the house." She turned to go.

"Don't forget to blow out the candles."

"How did you know I had candles burning?"

Jolene's cheeks went hot, realizing her slip-up. "My kitchen window overlooks the lake house. I saw them glowing."

"Fantastic." Kiara's eyes rolled. "The online description said it was a 'quaint and private oasis.' I can see that was a gross misrepresentation. Just like everything else."

Jolene just smiled. "See you soon, roomie!"

Closing the door behind Kiara, she raced to the kitchen to get her phone from its charging station. She dialed quickly.

"Pick up. Pick up."

"Hey sis." Rose's cheery voice answered on the other end of the line. "What's up?"

"Oh, you know, same ol', same ol'. Except for the fact I've suddenly got Luke's ex bunking with me for the night."

A laugh erupted through the phone. "Seriously? You can't make this stuff up! Only you, my dear, only you."

"That's not super encouraging, Rosie. I called you because I need a pep talk. A big one."

"Let me think." There was a long pause. "Sorry, Jojo. I don't seem to have 'how to survive a slumber party with current boyfriend's ex-girlfriend' in my pep talk repertoire."

Jolene looked out the kitchen window. One by one, she could see each candle extinguish. She knew she only had a few minutes to gather her composure. "He's not my boyfriend and she's technically his ex-fiancé."

"Wow. I *cannot* wait to hear about this tomorrow!"

"You're not helping," Jolene said. "In fact, you're making things worse. I'm actually sweating over here, sis. Like I just ran a marathon level of perspiration." She felt suddenly ill. "I bet Kiara doesn't even sweat. She's the type of woman that just glows. Or sparkles. She's almost perfect."

"Almost? What makes her not quite live up to that title?"

"The fact that she left a man like Luke."

"And yet you keep saying he's not your boyfriend."

"He's not," Jolene asserted, her words cut off by the knock at the door. "Oh shoot! She's back. Say a prayer for me, Rosie!"

"I pray that my sister has a fantastic story to tell me tomorrow morning, full of hilarity and embarrassing moments that will be the fodder of family jokes for many, many years to come."

"You are the worst," Jolene groaned.

"Love you too, sis!"

Jolene clicked off the phone call and hurried to the door.

"I was beginning to think you weren't going to answer," an irritated Kiara said, a scowl fixed on her face. She held the same bag Jolene had seen her with earlier in the day. "Can you please show me to my room?"

Stepping to the side, Jolene led Kiara to the guest room at the back of the house. She was grateful she'd remembered to wash the sheets after her sister's stay. At least Kiara wouldn't be able to complain about dog hair on the linens. She grabbed a clean towel from the top shelf of the closet and set it down on the foot of the bed.

"Just let me know what time you'd like to take a shower so we can coordinate. It takes the water heater about an hour to heat back up after use."

"Of course it does," Kiara quipped.

Ignoring her grumble, Jolene continued, "I usually make coffee in the morning if you'd like some. Regular or decaf?"

"Regular is fine."

Unzipping her bag, Kiara pulled out a dress and placed it on a hanger in the closet. Jolene stood in the doorframe, watching her without meaning to be intrusive but she figured it came across that way. Kiara seemed like the type of woman who always assumed the worst.

"I'll just let you get settled in, then. Let me know if you need anything."

"Thank you."

It was the first semi-nice thing Kiara said and Jolene embraced it. She had to give her the benefit of the doubt about something. She couldn't be all bad.

Calling Ace to join her, Jolene found her place on the couch again. The movie was one she'd already seen, but she found comfort in that. Anyway, her mind was too jumbled to really pay any attention to what was on the screen. She buried down under a plush blanket and tried to get lost in the movie.

At half past ten, Jolene heard the guest room door creak

open. She must've dozed off because her brain was muddled when she saw Kiara walk into the family room, wearing the same reindeer flannels pants she had on.

"Mind if I join you?" Kiara asked. She sat at the opposite end of the couch. "Nice jammies."

"Oh, sure. Of course." Jolene scooted over more, even though she was already at the edge of the cushion. "And thanks. They're my favorite."

"Mine too. They're the only ones that get softer with each wash."

"I know, right?" Jolene agreed excitedly. "I've tried so many other pairs but always come back to these ones."

Kiara smiled. "Want to know a secret?" She leaned closer. "I sometimes even wear them *after* Christmas."

"I don't retire this pair to the dresser drawer until well past Valentine's day!"

Kiara laughed. She had a beautiful laugh, a melodic one. "Do you mind if I watch with you?" She glanced to the television. "Had trouble sleeping."

"Not at all. I've seen this one before, but it's a good one. Spoiler alert—they fall in love."

Kiara grabbed the other corner of the blanket and slid under it. "I think I've seen them all, too, but it doesn't make me love them any less. Something so wonderfully reassuring about the consistency."

"Agreed."

Kiara looked like she was thinking about something, but if she was, she didn't say.

At the end of the movie, just after the much anticipated sweet kiss, Jolene looked over at Kiara and swore she saw her swipe a tear from the corner of her eye.

"Still just as good as the first time I saw it," Jolene said quietly.

"At one point in time, my life could've been one of these movies. That perfect fairytale." Kiara sighed deeply. "But I had to go and ruin it."

Jolene wondered whether or not she should let Kiara know just how much she knew about her failed relationship with Luke. To not say anything felt like lying, an omission of truth through silence.

"You know Luke and I were engaged, right? The man who's been staying next door?" Jolene nodded slowly. Kiara continued, "This was supposed to be our honeymoon week. We had plans to have this big winter wedding. I was going to ride in on my gray dappled mare and we would say our vows in front of his family's barn, just like his parents and grandparents all had. We hired this incredibly expensive caterer and put down deposits on all the rentals. It was going to break the bank, but it was going to be absolutely beautiful. Everything I'd ever dreamed of."

Kiara's description was so much more than Jolene had been able to imagine on her own, and she'd spent quite a long portion of the evening doing just that.

"It could've been in a movie," Kiara said wistfully. "The perfect setting. The perfect dress. The perfect man. But I had to go and make a perfectly stupid decision that would forever change everything. If I could go back to that point in time and take it back, I would. Absolutely."

"That's why you're here, then?" Jolene asked. "To work things out with Luke?"

Kiara didn't answer. Jolene could see she'd clearly overstepped. She clicked the television off. The glow of the Christmas tree reflected tiny white star-like dots on the walls and ceiling, adding a little warmth to an otherwise cold conversation.

"What do you do for living, Jolene?" Kiara swiftly

changed the subject. "Must be pretty successful to own a waterfront property like this."

Jolene's throat felt thick. "I just help maintain the lake house for now." She couldn't figure out what prompted her to, but she began to open up. "My fiancé passed away five years ago and life kind of turned upside down after that. All of my plans sort of went out the window and I've yet to gather them back up."

Clearly, that wasn't the answer Kiara had anticipated. "I'm so sorry."

"It's alright. It actually feels good to share that. Most people already know—those who live here, at least. But I haven't talked about it with anyone new in quite a while. I've wanted to." Her thoughts went to Luke. "I used to have dreams of opening up my own store. Nothing big—just an idea for a small little place on Glenn. I just love our little downtown and wanted to be a bigger part of it. I'd built a business plan and had a large amount in savings for startup costs. But after Mark died, it just never felt like a good time to chase that dream."

"Sometimes it's easier to dream when someone else is dreaming with you," Kiara said, like she was speaking from experience. "I take it you've been living off of your savings this whole time?"

Jolene hugged one of the throw pillows to her chest. "That and the little bit the O'Connells pay me. I don't live an extravagant life, so it's all I need for now."

"By the looks of things, I would guess a large chunk of your budget goes to pay for all of this holiday décor," Kiara teased, glancing around the room. "You really seem to love Christmas."

"I do. I mean, I've always loved it, but it's meant more to me these last few years. Mark passed at the first part of

December and I had two options—give up all hope or choose to find hope in something truly meaningful." Jolene swallowed tightly. "And what better to hope in than the gift of heaven coming down to earth?"

Kiara smiled.

"Anyway. Someday I'll dream my own dream, but for now I'm happy to help my friends realize theirs." Jolene picked up the television remote. "Want to watch another?"

"I probably shouldn't. I'm meeting Luke tomorrow and I'd prefer to not look like a walking zombie. I should head to bed again."

At the sound of his name, Jolene's stomach flipped.

"Goodnight, Jolene. Thank you again for letting me crash here tonight. I'm not sure what I would've done if you didn't have the room available."

"It's no problem," she replied. "One question. Do you mind me asking where Luke is staying tonight?"

"He said with his friend Roger just down the street."

Jolene smiled that Luke called Roger a friend, knowing he genuinely meant it. "Night, Kiara. Let me know if you need any extra blankets or anything. That back room can get a little drafty."

"Your home is just perfect, Jolene. Plus, I've got an adorable fluff ball to snuggle with if I do get cold."

18

LUKE

"ROGER, MY FRIEND, I need your advice on women."

Luke sat across from Roger at an old pine table in the kitchen. Roger's cabin was even smaller than the lake house and felt lived-in and cozy, with checkered red and white window coverings that matched the couch and the wallpaper and even the napkins folded on the table. It was as though Roger had picked one color-scheme and ran with it. Luke appreciated the uniformity and simplicity.

"Not sure I have all too much knowledge in that department."

"I don't know about that. Correct me if I'm wrong, but don't you and Mildred have a little something going on?"

"Millie's my sweetie." He laughed to himself. "Is it that obvious?"

"No," Luke assured, but he wasn't being completely honest. "I only picked up on it because I thought I caught a glimpse of you two holding hands on the carriage ride."

Roger blushed. "I'd told her to grab a pair of gloves but

she didn't listen. Her hands were like ice cubes. She's a stubborn one, that Millie."

Mildred was obstinate, Luke had already noticed that. In
a way, it surprised him that a man as kind and caring as
Roger would be drawn to someone with Mildred's more
challenging disposition. He seemed like such a good man,
and Mildred, well, in truth, she seemed like a cranky
old lady.

"You're wondering why I like her," Roger said, like he
could read Luke's mind. "I know she's not the easiest woman
to get along with. I know a lot of people in town say some
not-so-nice things about her. But you know what? She's got
the prettiest laugh. You've probably never heard it—it takes
a lot to actually get it out of her. But when I'm able to say
something that tickles her fancy and I get a little giggle from
her, well, it's just the sweetest sound in all the world. Like
jingle bells."

Luke rubbed his hands together for warmth. He noticed
the fire dwindling and that it needed a few more logs
thrown on to keep the flame going. He made a mental note
to gather a bundle from the cord of firewood along the side
of the house after Roger went to bed. He'd already been
instructed not to lift a finger. That he was a guest. Luke
wondered how often Roger had visitors other than Mildred
and Jolene.

"You got family, Roger?" he asked. He was curious if
Roger had always lived alone. Maybe he was the perpetual
bachelor that Luke figured he'd one day become. Didn't
seem so bad, though. Roger had a life that Luke admired,
one full of friends and love.

"I've got a daughter, Chelsea, who lives back east. Three
grown granddaughters and the best son-in-law on the
planet. I get to see them every year or so, but the older they

get, the busier their schedules are with their own families. It's hard for me to travel out to see them as often as I'd like." He nudged his glasses. "Doris, my wife, passed away during childbirth, so it was just Chelsea and me from the get-go."

"I'm so sorry to hear that, Roger. I had no idea."

"Of course you didn't, son. How could you have?" Roger replied, almost lightheartedly. "We don't wear life's tragedies for everyone to see, now do we? Suppose it would make life a little easier on us all if we did, though. It would sure give us a lot more grace with one another if we could get just a small glimpse of what others have gone through." He wrung his crinkled hands together, one over the other. "People like my Millie wouldn't be judged so harshly, I'm certain of that."

There was so much truth in that statement that Luke had to pause just to let it all sink in. Everyone had their own stories—their own joys and their own grief. No one was immune from life's hardships, but no one was without reason to celebrate, either. It seemed to Luke that many of the Merrylark residents he'd met so far had found the perfect balance for that.

"Anyway, it's getting too late for this old geezer. Now, just what was your question about women?"

Luke looked at the clock. It read half past ten. "It can wait until tomorrow. I should get to bed myself. Thanks again for letting me stay here, Roger. It's greatly appreciated. From picking me up on the highway to giving me a place to rest my head, you've sure come to my rescue these last few days."

"That's what friends are for." Rising slowly, Roger stood from the table and shuffled to the front door. He grabbed a scarf from the hall tree hook and wrapped it twice around his neck. "I'm going to get some more wood for the fire before I retire for the evening." He lifted a halting hand when Luke started to get up from his chair to assist him. "Just sit right back down, son. There are some tasks a man needs to do for himself to still feel like a man. Building his own fire is one of them."

"I'm not going to argue with you on that," Luke said as he lowered back down. "Just holler if you need some help, though. No shame in taking it."

Roger waved Luke off again and opened the front door, letting in a rush of cold that swirled around the house. Shivering, Luke rubbed his biceps with his palms. He couldn't wait to curl up under that plush blanket spread over the back of the couch. Roger had offered up his room, but Luke couldn't accept it. In fact, he was actually looking forward to crashing on the couch in the living room. It reminded him of the Christmases back when he was a kid and would sleep on the sofa. Even with his eyes shut, he could see the glimmer of the twinkling tree lights behind his eyelids. He always dreamt of Christmas morning on those nights, the tree's glow carrying into his dreams like some sort of holiday magic. It bothered Luke when his dad would have a fire in the fireplace on those nights. Didn't he know that Santa would be coming down the chimney? His father had assured him that Santa wore thick soled boots that could withstand the heat. Plus, after spending a year at the North Pole, surely he appreciated the extra warmth.

Luke smiled to himself.

"All set." Roger stumbled back into the house, a bundle of logs tucked under his arm. His shoulders were coated with a powdery dusting of white snow. "Starting to come down out there. If it keeps up, we might have to dig your truck out of the driveway in the morning. Forecasters said we could get up to a foot."

"Wouldn't that be something." Luke's voice was tinged with awe.

"Don't get a lot of snow in your neck of the woods?" Roger pulled the metal curtain back from the fireplace and placed a log on the top of the dwindling fire. The new piece popped and sizzled loudly.

"Don't get any snow, actually. We're in the valley so the most we ever get is an impressive hailstorm. Decent sized, though. One time one hit my grandma's car and as she would tell the story, that piece of hail was the size of a golf ball."

"So you've never experienced a white Christmas?"

"Not unless you count the year my dad accidentally put the liquid dishwashing soap in the dishwasher. We had fluffy white bubbles clear out to our living room."

Roger shook his head, laughing. "Sounds like something my Millie would do."

Luke liked the way Roger called her 'his Millie.'

"So tell me what we can we do to convince you to hang around long enough to experience a true Merrylark White Christmas?"

"That's still a couple weeks away, Roger. I've only got the lake house rented for three more days," Luke answered.

"I'm sure we could find a place for you. You could sleep on my couch for as long as you like. It's all yours."

"That's awfully nice, but I do have a life to get back to."

"It's a shame that you've created one here, then," Roger teased. "I know I don't just speak for myself when I say we've all become pretty fond of you, Handley."

"The feeling's mutual. That Merrylark magic everyone talks about has cast its spell on me."

"Magic." Roger tilted his head and shrugged. "Love. Same difference."

Hearing that four letter word made the hair on Luke's neck stand on end. He wasn't falling in love, was he? There was no way. Four days wasn't long enough to feel that way about someone.

But there was no other word to describe his growing feelings for Jolene. He was way passed just merely liking her. In fact, at this point, he'd never felt this way about anyone. Not even Kiara.

Kiara.

She hadn't been thrilled when he'd told her tonight wouldn't be a good night to talk after all. He'd ended things on such a beautiful note with Jolene that the last thing he wanted was for Kiara to spoil that. Whatever she needed to speak with him about would have to wait until the next day. It had already waited six months. One more sleep wouldn't be a big deal.

"I can see my mention of a certain word has gotten you dreaming," Roger said, pulling Luke from his thoughts. "That, or it's past your bedtime."

"Maybe a little of both," Luke admitted, yawning. "I should probably try to get some sleep."

"Same here. I feel a little silly admitting it, but it's about five hours past my bedtime," Roger said. "I usually get up around six to do my devotions. You're more than welcome to join me if you'd like. I'd love the company."

"That would be really nice, Roger. Appreciate the invite."

"Always, son."

※

"WAKE UP, HANDLEY!"

Luke felt his shoulders jostle roughly against the couch cushions.

"Handley, wake up!"

Slowly rising from slumber was not a luxury afforded to Merrylark visitors. For the third day in a row, Luke awoke with a startle.

"Roger?" Luke shaded his eyes against the glare of sunlight streaming across the lake and through the living room window. "Roger, what is it?"

"My Millie!" His voice shook with emotion. "There's been an accident. We have to go!"

❄

IT ONLY TOOK five minutes for Luke to shovel last night's snow from the driveway and double that for the two men to make it to the hospital just outside of town. Luke had called Jolene on their way to see if she needed a ride, but she was already in the waiting room.

She handed Luke a Styrofoam cup as soon as they walked through the automatic doors. "They just took her back."

"Millie!" Roger stood up on toe, panic flashing in his eyes. "Millie!"

"Roger." Jolene placed her hands on Roger's shoulders. "They're checking her out now. We just need to wait."

Pulling out from her grip, Roger sidestepped around Jolene. "I have to get to her. I have to see her."

"They're only letting family in. We have to wait here."

"But she doesn't have any family," Roger said, weakly. A tear slid down his cheek and over his trembling chin. "We're her family."

Jolene rubbed her old friend's back. "I know." With one guiding hand, she led him to the row of plastic chairs along the waiting room wall. After settling him down, she came over to Luke, out of Roger's earshot.

"What happened?" Luke whispered. He took a sip of the hot coffee in his hands.

"One of the cats got out this morning when Millie opened the door to get the paper. Apparently when she tried to run after it, she slipped on a patch of ice on the stoop. Hit her head pretty good and banged up her wrist. They're going to run some tests and take a couple x-rays."

"Poor Millie." Luke felt just awful for her. "Did she find her cat?"

Jolene frowned. "That's the worst part. Poor thing got hit by a car just outside her house. Millie doesn't know that, though. The paramedics said they saw a cat on the side of the road when they were bringing her in. I don't have the heart to tell her. I'm still holding out hope it wasn't hers."

Luke knew just how much Mildred loved her cats. "That's terrible." He glanced over his shoulder to Roger who sat in his chair, shoulders sagging and eyes wet with tears. "Do they have any idea how long it'll be before we hear anything?"

"My guess is an hour or so. They rushed her right in. All we can do now is wait."

For the next hour, the three passed the time with several rounds of gin rummy. Roger won all four hands, but it didn't cheer him up any. The fatigue of worry finally caught up to him after the last hand and he closed his eyes, resting his head on Jolene's shoulder. Luke sat on the other side and out of his periphery he could see her murmur something quietly in her friend's ear, but he couldn't hear it.

The corner of Roger's mouth lifted into the faintest smile.

Getting up from her seat, Jolene took off her jacket,

folded it, and placed it on the chair next to Roger, creating a makeshift bed for her friend to get some rest. She helped get him situated and then returned to her chair next to Luke.

Luke took Jolene's hand into his.

She turned her head, smiling. "Thank you for bringing him."

"Of course. I'm glad you called." Luke rubbed his thumb against the back of Jolene's hand. Her skin was so smooth, so soft. "How'd you know I was staying at Roger's?"

"Kiara told me last night during our slumber party."

Luke's thumb stopped moving. "Come again?"

"Kiara stayed over last night. The power's completely out at the lake house. Remind me to have you check that out later." Jolene leaned into him as she interjected that request. "She told me you were at Roger's."

This information wasn't something Luke could readily process. He tried to conceal his shocked expression.

"We watched a few holiday movies and chatted about life for a bit. She's actually quite lovely, Luke. And Ace is really fond of her. In fact, Kiara asked if she could take him for a run this morning." She looked at her watch. "Bet they're out on that run right about now."

Luke was astonished. He had no clue how to respond but felt an apology of some sort was appropriate. "I'm so sorry for that, Jolene. You should've called me. I would've dealt with her."

"It was really no big deal, Luke. I actually enjoyed her company. She was a bit cold at first, but quickly warmed up." Laughing to herself, Jolene clarified, "Her personality, that is. Though I suppose she *was* freezing without the heater and all."

"I honestly don't know what to say, Jolene." Luke shook his head. "I'm completely in awe of you."

"Because I let someone stay in a spare room that just so happened to be vacant? Definitely not Mother Theresa status. I just did what anyone would do in that situation. My neighbor needed help, so I offered it."

"I don't think you realize how incredible you are."

"I'm hardly incredible—"

"You are *absolutely* incredible."

Something changed in Jolene's gaze, making Luke's heart stutter. Blinking, Jolene looked up at him, lips parted. With her hand still in his, Luke slowly leaned in, bringing their foreheads together, just so they barely touched. He breathed out. Jolene's eyes drifted closed. So did Luke's.

"Roger Wilkins?"

Jolene bolted upright, jumping from her chair. She dropped Luke's hand like it was on fire. "Here!" she blurted. "I mean, he's right here." She hurried over to Roger to jostle him awake. "Roger, they're calling for you."

"Millie? Is my Millie okay?" A sleepy and disoriented Roger sat up.

The nurse rushed to his side and took hold of his arm. "She's asking for you, sir. Right this way."

Arms linked with the nurse, Roger shuffled out the door.

Luke looked over at Jolene, but the moment their eyes met, she turned around. He'd wanted to kiss her so many times, but this was the first time he'd ever acted on that impulse.

Standing, he came to her side. "Jolene—"

"That's a good sign that she's asking for Roger, right? That they're letting her have visitors already? That has to be good."

"I would think so," Luke agreed.

"I just feel so terrible for Roger. What a crazy morning. All of that worry can't be good for his heart."

With her statement, Luke realized just how little he knew about his new friends. "Does he have a bad heart?"

"Had a heart attack three years ago while unloading his Christmas tree from the back of his truck. Millie's the one who found him. She was out walking one of her cats—"

"Wait one second—she walks her cats?"

"Yep, on a leash and everything. It's actually pretty impressive," Jolene explained. "Anyway, she found him and gave CPR to revive him. Mouth to mouth and all. Can you believe it? When Roger woke up, he said that he'd been waiting to kiss Millie for two years and if having a heart attack was what it took to get it, he'd have one all over again."

"That sounds like Roger." Luke chuckled. "He really does like her, doesn't he?"

"I think it's a bit more than like at this point."

They both knew the word she was referring to, but neither of them could say it, even if it was about someone else entirely.

Luke felt the need to clear the air. "Listen, Jolene. I didn't mean to—"

"It's okay, Luke. I read things wrong, and for that, I'm sorry."

"You're not reading anything wrong, Jolene. I've wanted to k—"

"I like Kiara," Jolene interrupted. "I think you guys would be really great together if you could work out your differences. It's worth a shot. She seems like a genuinely nice person who really cares about you."

"It's more than just differences, Jolene. And it's not something I even want to work out."

Like she didn't hear a word he'd said, Jolene said wistfully, "Who am I to get in the way of true love?"

He wanted to tell her that she was getting in the way of her own true love, but a page over the hospital intercom asking Jolene to report to the front desk interrupted him.

"I'll go find out what's going on," she said. "Be right back."

It was like Jolene couldn't hurry away fast enough. Luke wondered what it would take to convince her that he and Kiara were a thing of the past. It was as though she couldn't accept the very clear fact that Jolene was the only woman he was interested in.

Had he been too forward in trying to kiss her? It felt like the moment had been leading up to it, the way her eyelashes fluttered up at him expectantly. How she scooted in. It was only an inch or two, but it felt like they were being drawn to one another, some magnetic pull. He knew she felt it too. It would've been impossible not to.

Just a few moments later, Jolene walked back into the waiting room, her usual smile on her face.

"They're going to keep her overnight," she said. "Said they couldn't find anything too concerning but they'd like to monitor her for just a while longer. Roger's going to stay. I told him I'd bring by a change of clothes later this evening, but for now, we're good to go."

"That's all great to hear. I bet Roger is breathing a huge sigh of relief," Luke said, tossing his empty coffee cup into a nearby wastebasket. "If you're ready to go, I can give you a ride."

"I'd love that," she said. Her shoulders relaxed and she took a deep breath. "What a morning, right?"

"You could say that again," Luke agreed.

"This town sure keeps me on my toes. Too bad poor Millie couldn't manage to stay on hers."

Luke laughed. Jolene was so smart, beautiful, witty. Kind

and caring. Generous. All of the things he'd been looking for in a woman and many of the things he didn't even know to look for.

He'd thought this whole time that Merrylark itself was magical, but he was beginning to think Jolene was the real reason for it all. She was the magic.

19

JOLENE

"DID YOU FIND the tail?"

Holding the brown cardboard box out at arm's length, Luke shook his head. His nose scrunched in disgust. "Nope. But I have to confess—I didn't spend much time looking. In fact, I'm not even one hundred percent sure it's a cat. There's a very good chance this is a possum or raccoon in here, but I'm not brave enough to open it back up to double check."

Laughing, Jolene finished writing the day's date on a small piece of wood. She stapled a stake to the back of it. It was a makeshift headstone, but it would have to do. She hoped Millie wouldn't be too particular.

"I'm pretty sure it was Ozzy that got out," Jolene said, second guessing herself now that she looked at his name written on the sign. "I honestly can't keep track of all her cats."

"Here's to hoping Millie can't, either." Luke gestured toward the box containing the unidentifiable animal in his hands. "Shall we go have a proper burial?"

"This is anything but proper, but it feels like the right

thing to do. I'd hate for her to have to deal with this when she gets home. I'm sure Roger would take care of it for her, but I'd rather he only take care of Millie. He'll have enough on his plate."

Luke nodded. It felt like the least they could do. He followed Jolene out Millie's front door, careful not to let any other cats sneak out as he shut the door behind them. Millie's house didn't back up to the water like many of the other Merrylark homes. Instead, she had a small fenced in yard with a flower garden that had gone dormant for the winter, but still had yard ornaments stuck in the ground, spaced out evenly within the planters. There was a metal daisy that had white petals that spun around with a gust of wind, like a pinwheel. Luke smiled and Jolene noticed his reflective expression. She was glad for Luke to see this side of Millie and hoped that something about the scene endeared Millie to him more. Jolene hoped that getting a deeper glimpse into Millie's life and the things she cared about would make Luke realize she was more than just a cranky old woman—that she had layers and under the ornery ones was a woman with a truly decent heart.

Next to the planter was a carved stone statue of a cat curled up like it was sleeping by a fire, its tail wrapped all the way around his body. Jolene figured this was Millie's cat cemetery. Honestly, it creeped her out a bit but she had to remind herself that Luke likely buried his horses on his property back home, and nothing about that seemed weird to her. Everyone had their own way of handling things.

Luke handed off the cat casket to Jolene and reached for a shovel propped against the side of the house. He began to dig through the fresh layer of snow just a few feet from the statue. Jolene hoped he wouldn't accidentally uncover any other cat remains.

"I feel like we should say a few remarks," Jolene said, eyeing the box warily. "Like a eulogy or tribute. Don't you think?"

"I s'pose so. I've never buried a cat before, let alone one I'd never met."

"I know. Me neither." She closed her eyes and angled her face heavenward. "Ollie—I mean Ozzy," she quickly corrected, "was a good cat. A fluffy one. He liked to sleep and eat and scratch up the furniture, but Millie didn't mind. She loved him all the more for it. I don't know why he tried to escape this cold December morning, but my guess is that he was on his way to rally all of the town's strays in hopes of bringing them back to live a life full of Millie's love, just as he had. It was a selfless act that led to poor Ozzy's fateful end. He was a martyr—a true cat martyr."

Luke snickered but Jolene continued her prayer.

"May Ozzy have an eternity filled with unlimited sand-boxes to do his business in and endless amounts of catnip to keep him feeling frisky," she said in closing.

Jolene opened her eyes and crouched down. Luke had carved out a big enough hole for the box to fit in, and she easily placed the box into the ground. Grabbing a handful of unearthed dirt from the pile next to her, she sprinkled it over the cardboard lid and crossed herself.

"Rest in peace, Ozzy."

"Rest in peace," Luke echoed.

He covered the hole back up and then took a shovel full of snow to spread on top. Jolene then drove the stake head-stone into the ground and stepped back, arms folded over her chest.

"I feel better." She looked at Luke. "Do you feel better?"

"I think so."

"I sure hope that was Ozzy," Jolene said, contemplatively. "I'll feel awful if it's a different one of her cats in that box."

"Whoever or whatever it was, it got the best burial any piece of road kill has ever gotten, that I'm sure of."

"Very true." Jolene shivered and tugged her wool jacket tighter across her body. "Gosh, it's getting cold. Want to go into town with me to warm up with some of Martha's sweets? I have a huge craving for some shortbread."

Putting his arm around her shoulders, Luke said, "It feels like the only appropriate thing to do after a cat burial."

"You're not making fun of me, are you?" She elbowed his ribs.

"Absolutely not. I would love nothing more than to drown my sorrows in sugar."

"That's the only way to do it!"

❄

MARTHA DROPPED A paper bag onto the center of the table.

"These are all of our day-olds. On the house," she said with a wink. She swiped her hands against her apron and blew a breath that lifted her gray hair from her forehead. "Enjoy! I've got to get back to baking!"

Opening up the bag, Jolene peered in. "All of this is left over from yesterday?"

"Oh sweetie, that's not even the tip of the iceberg. You would be amazed how much goes in the dumpster each night. Easily ten times that."

"And you can't just resell them the next day? I'd pay good money for these." Jolene took a snickerdoodle out of the bag and bit off a piece. It was mouthwatering—maybe not quite as soft as usual—but the flavor was unmatched and it tasted every bit as delicious as Martha's other baked creations.

"Absolutely not!" Martha looked horrified. "When people come into The Rolling Pin, they expect something fresh, gooey, and right out of the oven. I would never feel right selling anything less than just that! Plus, we don't have any extra room in our pastry cases. Doesn't make any sense to hang onto them."

Luke took the bag and rummaged through it. "Too bad there isn't a place, I don't know—*maybe down the street*—that is big enough for all of this and more so it didn't have to go to waste."

Martha got the hint. "I've told Devon I've no interest in that retail space of his. There's no place in it for a proper kitchen to accommodate the huge ovens we have here. Sure, sometimes I do wish I had more room for the customers to stay and enjoy their purchases, but I've already got a baker's dream kitchen. I'd never give that up." She nodded toward the back of the store. "I do hate to waste so much, but nothing else makes any sense. Anyway, you two enjoy and I'll be back in a bit to check on you."

Left to their bag of sweets, Jolene and Luke continued the conversation about Devon's retail store. Jolene understood Martha's reasoning. The Rolling Pin had been in the same spot on Glenn Street for over twenty-five years, and she figured the thought of starting out on a brand new venture at Martha and Gary's age was a daunting one. It wasn't for Jolene, though. It was exciting to think of a new endeavor, new possibilities. It reminded her of the excitement she once had for her little shop that never was. But she couldn't push someone to do something they didn't fully get behind. New businesses already had such low success and survival rates, even with enthusiastic entrepreneurs leading the way. What Martha said made sense.

"I still believe the town could use another place like this," she told Luke as she looked out the window wistfully. "A place to come together. To relax and recharge. Almost like a hub for our little town."

"I agree," Luke said. "But it doesn't sound like anything Martha's going to take on without some convincing. And then there's the whole coffee part. I can't imagine Cat would appreciate the competition."

"She wouldn't have any," Jolene said around a mouthful of banana muffin. If she didn't watch herself, she'd consume the entire bag of pastries. "Cat would give up the truck for a retail location in a heartbeat. The only reason she even has the truck is because there wasn't any space available back when she started her business. I know she hates hauling that thing all over town. If she could settle into a storefront, I'm sure she would." She sighed. "If only these sorts of things were free."

"Well, dreaming is free and planning is free, so I don't think we should stop doing either of those two things. Might be worth a conversation with Cat. We should ask if she has some time available later on today so we can find out what page she's on."

"You've had a conversation with Cat before, haven't you? We won't need any time at all—we'll know within the first five minutes!"

❄

"I LOVE IT!"

No sooner were the words out of Jolene's mouth than Cat was clapping her hands enthusiastically like she was keeping time in a church choir. A quick phone call to Cat after Jolene's earlier conversation with Luke led to an impromptu meeting at The Rolling Pin, just as the two were finishing up their midmorning snack. Coincidentally, Cat had been doing a little holiday shopping on Glenn Street and had a free moment to join them.

"Sign me up!" she shouted, her voice echoing in the small bakery.

"I wish it was that simple," Jolene said, wanting to bring Cat down from her excitement gently. "I mean, you do have all we need on the coffee end of things, but then there's fixtures and tables and chairs. Permits and licenses. Things like that. It doesn't sound like a lot, but it all adds up quickly. Luke and I ran some numbers and our conservative guess to get the place to where it would need to be is around sixty thousand."

Cat nodded. "I'm actually not too surprised by that. Startup money was a huge barrier for entry back when I got the truck. Sweetie," she took Jolene's hands into hers across the table, "I would love nothing more than to be business partners with you, but those figures are a little cost prohibitive, what with college coming up in a few years for Tanner and all. Unless Santa delivers a huge sack of cash under my Christmas tree this year, I fear it'll just have to remain a far off dream. Doesn't hurt to dream though, right?"

Something sank within Jolene's heart. Part of her had known all along that this crazy idea wouldn't work out— that it was a harebrained hope with no real financial footing. It was beginning to feel like she'd squandered everything over the last five years when she'd lived off her savings. She shouldn't have done that; she should've gotten a real job and left the money untouched. She'd thought she'd been helping her friends out by volunteering rather than asking for pay, but in doing so, she'd forfeited the ability to actually help these same friends realize their own dreams, and that was the worst feeling of all.

After saying their goodbyes to Cat, Jolene and Luke walked toward the truck. Luke had lunch plans with Kiara and that fact didn't help lighten Jolene's spirits any. For the first time during this particular holiday season, Jolene felt utterly hopeless. She couldn't muster any cheer to speak of.

The streets were crowded, shoppers with colorful bags dodging one another while keeping clear of snowy patches that lined the walkways. Water droplets dripped from gutters overhead. Every time a store door would open, the warbling sound of chatter, cash registers, and customers would spill out onto the streets. While it was usually a heart-warming atmosphere, today it felt like a cacophony of chaos.

Jolene's eyes stung with tears.

"Hey." Luke said, bumping her shoulder with his. "You okay?"

Sniffing, Jolene shrugged. "Yeah, I'm fine. It's just been an emotional morning. First with Millie and then talking with Cat. I don't now—I think I just feel a little let down. Defeated in a way. I'm sorry."

"It's perfectly okay to admit you're disappointed, Jolene. You're allowed that."

"I know I am. I just don't like to be a downer."

"That is not a word I would *ever* use to describe you. The opposite, in fact. But it's not your job to cheer everyone up. I know you think it is, but you're only one person and you're allowed to have bad days, too. Entitled to them, even."

She knew he was right, but she didn't like to admit it.

"How about you let me help turn your day around? Just

because it started off not so great doesn't mean it needs to end that way."

Jolene perked up, if only a little. "What do you have up your sleeve, Luke Handley?"

"Oh, just a little something, but you'll have to wait to find out," Luke said as he gave her shoulder a light squeeze. "Be ready at seven o'clock and wear your warmest winter gear. Maybe that Olympian sponsored sub-zero jacket of yours."

And with that, just a small sliver of hope returned within Jolene and she knew she had Luke to thank for it.

20

LUKE

LUKE WAS EAGER for his lunch with Kiara, if only for the fact that after it he could send her merrily on her way back down the mountain to Kernlyville. She'd thrown a huge monkey wrench in his ranch hand respite just by showing up in Merrylark. His main goal in staying at the lake house for the week was to relax and take his mind off of the tumultuous year he'd had. He wanted to finish out the season on a positive note, but that wasn't possible with Kiara around, requesting his attention. Whatever she needed to speak with him about, he prayed it would be a quick and relatively painless conversation, though conversations with Kiara were rarely those two things.

"Sorry I'm late!" Like a tumbleweed, Kiara swirled into the restaurant and slid into the red vinyl booth, tucking her purse next to her on the seat. She looked over her shoulder and surveyed the establishment. "This place is certainly...quirky."

"Sal's is the best."

That wasn't entirely true. The service was slow and the food just so-so. Luke felt a combative mood creeping up in him merely by being in Kiara's presence, and that wasn't exactly fair. He'd have to try a little harder to keep the peace.

Kiara picked up a menu. "Did you order already?"

"Yep. Got you a Cobb salad."

He wasn't sure why he'd ordered Kiara's meal for her. It had been their routine back when they were together and something in him—either instinct or familiarity—made him do it again without any real thought. "*She'll have the salad with nonfat dressing on the side. No croutons.*"

"Perfect. You always did know exactly what I liked." Kiara beamed at him. Her eyes crinkled at the corners in a way that seemed so sincere he couldn't make sense of it. Even still, Luke didn't trust it. Anyone could appear genuine by saying all the right things and smiling politely. However, actions were so much louder than words.

"Luke." She paused after saying his name, just staring at him. If he'd been eating, he would've thought he had something on his face. "Luke," she repeated, more softly.

"That's still my name."

"Listen, I know me showing up here is just about the *last* thing you expected."

"Just about."

"Honestly, I wasn't going to. I'd talked myself out of it close to a hundred times. But I knew this was the right thing to do, even if it was difficult to do it. Even if you didn't want to see me. Even if you *wouldn't* see me."

Luke wished she would've tried talking herself out of it just one more time. One hundred and one times might've been the magic number.

"I've made mistake after mistake in my life lately, Luke. But this—this is my attempt to change that." Reaching over, she unlatched her purse and pulled a white envelope from within it. She slid it across the table.

Seeing his name in her perfect handwriting made Luke swallow hard.

"You don't have to open it right now. In fact, I'd rather you not. But I wanted to get this into your hands and I figured if I mailed it, it would just end up in the trash."

"Probably so."

"See? I *do* know you, too, Luke." She was trying hard, Luke had to give her credit for that. "Anyway...I know it won't magically make everything right between us, but maybe it will help things feel a little less wrong."

"I'm not sure how that's possible, Kiara. You *left* me. I promised my life to you, and that wasn't enough. I'm not sure how anything in that envelope will change any of that. Unless it's some time machine where you can go back and redo the past, I honestly just don't see how it can fix anything. You hurt me, Kiara. A lot."

"I know," she said through silent tears that began to trickle down her rouged cheeks. She dabbed at them with her fingers. "I know I did."

"I loved you—at least it felt like love at the time." Luke shrugged. "I don't know. Deep down I know it's for the best that things turned out the way they did. At least I got to see your true colors *before* the wedding day."

"That's just the thing, Luke. Those aren't my true colors. At least I don't want them to be. I'm hoping what's in that envelope will help you see me in a different light."

It wasn't in Luke's nature to stay bitter. In truth, it had felt unnatural to hang onto his anger toward Kiara for this long. His heart wanted so badly to forgive her, if only so he could move on with his life without her hold on it. To be free of the hurt he experienced each time he thought of her.

"I'll read it." He picked up the envelope and tucked it

into his shirt pocket. "But I can't promise it will change anything."

"The fact that you were even willing to have this conversation already changes everything for me, Luke."

He didn't know how to interpret that so he was grateful for the distraction of their food brought to the table. He was halfway into his cheeseburger when he could feel Kiara's eyes on him without even needing to look up to verify. When he finally did lift his head, she was staring at him, almost dreamily.

"Doesn't this feel good, Luke? Just the two of us again, eating together like we used to. I mean, not necessarily at a restaurant like this particular one, but just being together, doesn't it bring back anything for you?"

"Kiara—"

"Don't you ever wonder what things would've been like if it had all worked out differently? Don't you ever think about us? What might've been?"

It bothered Luke how she spoke of their life together like she didn't have any say in their breakup.

"Kiara, I'm falling in love with someone else."

Kiara's eyes went wide. "Oh." She gulped. "Not what I was expecting."

"I wasn't expecting it either, but it's happening. In fact, falling is the wrong word. I'm *in* love with someone else," Luke said. He felt something unfurl in his chest by verbally acknowledging his feelings for Jolene. "She's kind and funny and wonderful and every time I learn something new about her, I find more reasons to love her." He reached for the envelope. "So maybe you should take this. I've moved on, and I'm really happy about that. I hope you can understand."

"No. No, you should keep it." Kiara nodded toward the

envelope. "I'm happy for you, Luke. I can't say I'm not jealous, but that's my problem, not yours," she admitted. "Do I happen to know the lucky lady?"

"Yeah. You've met her."

Kiara smiled. "Well, I hope she realizes just what she has in you, Luke. You deserve happiness. More than anyone."

"So do you, Kiara."

"I wouldn't be so quick to say that." Kiara shook her head. She pushed around a lettuce leaf in her bowl with her fork. "I deserve something, but it's not happiness."

"Kiara, I forgive you."

Kiara's head snapped up, her eyes colliding with Luke's. "You do?"

"I do. I don't think I realized it until just now, but I actually forgive you. For a long time, I wanted you to experience the kind of pain I felt when you called off our wedding, but being here this week has made me see things differently. There's no sense in holding on to anger. It doesn't do you any good and it sure doesn't do me any good."

"I can't tell you what a relief that is to hear, Luke. I never thought I'd hear those words from you. But I don't think I'm ready to forgive myself. Not yet. It doesn't feel right."

"Grace never does. It's unnatural. Unjust. But it feels really, really good to give it. You should try it."

Kiara sat back against the booth, looking at Luke with scrutiny. "This place has changed you," she said. "Not that you needed any changing, but it's brought something out in you that I don't remember from before."

"This place. These people." Looking out the restaurant window onto Glenn Street, Luke felt the pang of homesickness at the thought of leaving Merrylark in just two short days. "Honestly Kiara, I don't know how I'm ever going to leave."

"So don't."

"I'm beginning to feel like I won't be able to. I can't imagine life anywhere else."

"Any*where* else?" Kiara asked, her penciled eyebrow arching inquisitively. "Or *with* anyone else?"

"Both," Luke admitted.

"I know I'm probably the last person you want romantic advice from, but if you truly love this woman and see a future with her, then you need to do everything in your power to make things work." Kiara looked up as the waitress to came to refill the water glasses on the table. She waited until she left before saying, "Speaking from experience, if you don't, it just might be the biggest regret of your life."

Gathering her purse, Kiara pulled out her wallet and tossed a twenty-dollar bill onto the table. Luke didn't expect her to pay for her meal, but when he reached for his wallet, Kiara waved him off.

"I should get going. I'm heading back to the lake house to gather my things, but should be out of your hair by later this afternoon. Thank you again for meeting with me, Luke. I know it came as quite a surprise."

"You don't have to rush out of town, Kiara. You should stay and enjoy Merrylark. This place really is amazing."

"I don't doubt it is."

Luke slid out of his side of the booth to stand, leaning in to give Kiara a hug before she left. She held on longer than he would've, but he let it be, knowing this goodbye was more for her than it was for him. What he didn't expect, however, were her lips suddenly on his. It took his body a moment to react, not out of hesitation, but the pure shock of it locking him in place. Finally, snapping to his senses, he pushed away.

He wiped his mouth with the back of his hand.

"I'm so sorry, Luke," Kiara stammered. "Old habits die hard, I suppose."

It sounded more like an excuse than an apology, but he wasn't going to give her a hard time about it.

"It's okay, Kiara." He pressed forward for another hug, this time sure to release her quickly. "Take care, okay? And happy holidays."

"Happy holidays to you, too, Luke. Always."

With that, Kiara gathered her composure and her things and walked out of Sal's, glancing over her shoulder as she nudged the restaurant door open, throwing one last wave in the air as the final chapter of her life with Luke closed for good.

21

JOLENE

NORMALLY, JOLENE WOULD wear the same scarf throughout all of winter. Her only requirement was that it keep her neck warm, and if she found one that did that sufficiently, she'd wear it all the way into springtime.

But today she felt like searching for a new scarf, something to freshen up her tired wardrobe. She doubted Luke would even notice, but that was alright with her. Sometimes a girl just needed to treat herself.

Determined to bring a little more joy to her challenging morning, Jolene made a concerted effort to wear a smile on her face, even if she didn't necessarily feel like it. She'd found that sometimes you had to fake it until you made it, so she did just that as she walked down Glenn Street. With every returned smile from a neighbor or passerby, Jolene's own grin felt that much more genuine. By the time she opened the door to her favorite little clothing store, Ivy's Dress Shoppe, she was beaming.

"Jolene! Merry Christmas! Haven't seen you in ages!" Ivy, a tall redhead with a smattering of freckles across the bridge of her nose, shouted from behind the cash register. She stepped out to rush over to Jolene and wrap her in a hug. "What brings you in today? Can I help you find anything in particular?"

"Just looking for a new scarf, but I see you've gotten a store-full of new inventory since my last visit."

"We have. Mostly cocktail dresses for holiday parties and New Year's Eve, but I did just get a shipment of the softest gloves you will ever feel. One hundred percent cashmere. Come on over here and see for yourself." Ivy grabbed Jolene's wrist and led her to a display near the glass windows at the front of the store. Gloves of all colors and textures lined the tabletop, looking like frosted mitten sugar cookies lined up on a cookie sheet. Picking up a teal pair, Ivy slid one onto Jolene's hand. "See? Isn't that luxurious?"

Gloves weren't in Jolene's budget, but she couldn't resist the decadent feel of the ones on her hands. She opened and closed her fingers, wriggling them against the soft texture.

"These are pretty amazing," she agreed, tugging the glove from her fingers. She placed it back onto the table after reading the price tag. "But unfortunately, a bit out of my price range."

"Didn't you say you were looking for a scarf?" Ivy asked. "Well, today only is buy one scarf, get a pair of gloves for free!"

"And how come you don't have any signs advertising this incredible deal?" Jolene asked, her voice full of questioning.

"Oh, you know, it's not cost effective to make signs for flash sales like this."

"It's also not cost effective to give away such high-end gloves to your customers at no cost."

"Jolene, you're more than a customer. You're a friend. Remember that time a few years back when the flu was running rampant through town and all of my employees were out sick on Christmas Eve? If my memory serves me correctly, you came to the rescue and helped me hold down the fort so all of the procrastinators could do their last minute Christmas shopping. Don't believe I ever properly paid you for your time."

"Because I wouldn't've accepted it. I didn't have any other plans and was happy to spend the evening here with you. I just love how alive Glenn Street is on Christmas Eve. The carols, the buzz, the energy. It was fun to have a front row seat for it all."

Ivy smiled. Though she and Jolene weren't necessarily close, Jolene agreed that she would label her a friend. They'd had a great time that Christmas Eve night, blasting music from the store's sound system and dancing around the clothing racks. She never told Ivy, but it had been her first holiday without Mark. At first, she wasn't sure how she'd survive it, but working with Ivy that night had been the perfect distraction.

"You hang onto these." Ivy tucked the pair of gloves into Jolene's purse and grinned. "My gift to you. Now, to find the perfect coordinating scarf. Come on over here, I think I have just the one."

❄

JOLENE'S STEP FELT lighter as she walked up the street toward her car. She didn't have to manufacture a smile, a genuine one lit up her entire face. Ivy had paired the most lovely blue and purple floral scarf with the gloves and Jolene wore them both with pride, adoring the way they complimented her navy colored pea coat. She felt put together and beautiful, which was often hard to do with all of the layering these winter temperatures demanded.

Her car was just a block up, so she quickened her stride, knowing she only had about thirty minutes until Roger and Millie would be expecting her back at the hospital with Roger's things for the night. She'd touched base with the two earlier and as Roger described it, Millie was going stir crazy, eager to get back home and out of the confines of her hospital room. Even still, it was best for her to be there. It would put everyone at ease to have her monitored for just a bit longer.

Coming up on Sal's Diner on her right, Jolene had the idea to pop in quickly and grab some soup to take with her to the hospital. She knew hospital food could be less than appealing, and Thursdays at Sal's were chicken noodle soup. Nothing better for the soul than that!

She was just about to push open the door when she caught sight of Luke and Kiara through the window. They shared a meal and a look that made Jolene's stomach turn, like she was cresting the top of the roller coaster, hanging onto the edge right before making the spiraling descent. She swallowed hard.

Kiara stood first, then Luke. Jolene didn't like the fact that she was spying, but she couldn't pull her eyes away. When they embraced, Jolene felt cold in her bones, the scarf and gloves doing little to keep her from shivering.

Then the two kissed, right there in the middle of the lunch time rush in Sal's Diner. Jolene gasped, her chin trembling. It lasted longer than a cordial little peck should. From Jolene's perspective on the other side of the window, it felt like minutes passed before either pulled away.

Jolene spun around. She ran down the street, jostled by the shoulders that she bumped as though she was in the middle of an arcade pinball game. When she finally arrived at her car, her eyes were bleary with tears, her nose dripping and cold. She tugged on the door handle and collapsed into the driver's seat. Only then did she allow herself to completely fall apart.

❄

"I'LL KILL HIM." Millie scowled.

Jolene laughed through tears that hadn't let up since witnessing Luke and Kiara's kiss back at the restaurant.

"That's a bit dramatic, don't you think, sweetie?" Roger squeezed Millie's hand, mindful of the IV tubes taped to it. He sat right next to her bedside, as close as he could get without joining her under the thin hospital blanket.

"Not one bit. Stupid fool to hurt Jojo like that. And to plant one on that broad in broad daylight! At the very least, he deserves a wallop upside the head!"

"It's okay, really," Jolene said. She twirled her fork around the curly noodles in her Styrofoam cup. Even though she hadn't been able to get Sal's chicken noodle soup for her friends, she did stop back home to grab several instant soup cups on her way over. It wasn't homemade, but it did the job.

"It's absolutely not okay," Roger argued. "And it makes no sense whatsoever. Why on God's green earth would he kiss that woman?"

"Because he loves her."

"He does not."

"I honestly think he does," Jolene countered. "And I know she loves him. She never stopped."

"Well, she *must've* stopped because you don't just leave someone you're in love with."

That comment was like a sharp knife sunk right into Jolene's heart. Roger was right—you didn't leave someone you loved. That was just further confirmation that what she thought she felt with Luke wasn't love, at least not from his perspective. If it had been, it wouldn't have been so easy for him to kiss Kiara.

"There has to be an explanation for all of this. The Luke Handley I know would never do something like that," Roger reasoned.

"That's just the thing. I think we don't really know him, after all." Putting her soup down on the tray next to her, Jolene cupped her face, thumbing away the lines of salty tears streaking down her cheeks. "It was stupid for me to fall for him so quickly. I usually have better judgment than that. I've only got myself to blame for all of this, really. I'm just sorry to have dragged you all into it, too."

"You're being much too hard on yourself, dear," Roger offered, his eyes full of sympathy. "We were all fooled."

"Didn't fool me, that imposter. I knew from the beginning he was nothing but trouble."

"Did you, now?" Jolene challenged her friend.

"Yup, what with all those silly gray hairs and that stupid fake accent. Can't trust him, is what I originally told myself. Never trust a cowboy," Millie grumbled.

"Been burned by a cowboy in the past, sweetie?" Roger pushed his glasses to his nose with his finger. "This is a story I haven't heard."

"No story, I just don't trust a person who owns horses and not cows and is a man and not a boy. Nothing about that title makes any sense, if you ask me. Merrylark is better off without that Luke Handley character, no question about that."

Jolene couldn't say she agreed, but didn't have the energy to argue or even defend Luke's honor at that point. Something about that revelation made her disappointed with herself because she knew if the tables had been turned, Luke would likely come to her defense. But maybe that was just the Luke she wanted to believe existed. The one she saw back at the diner wouldn't do that. Would he?

"Anyhoo, how much longer they gonna keep me locked up in this prison cell? Two, three weeks?"

"You've only been here eight hours so far," Roger reasoned. "And we get to go home tomorrow."

"But the cats—"

"I've already been by the house to check on and feed them. All are doing well," Jolene assured. "I'll stop by again in the morning and refill their water and empty the litter boxes."

"What if Ozzy comes back and I'm not there to let him in? He'll freeze out there tonight, especially if that darn snow picks up again."

Jolene and Roger exchanged a knowing glance. "I'll keep an eye out for him. I'm sure he's found a nice, toasty place to hunker down. He's got a built in fur coat, Millie. He'll be just fine."

She didn't have the heart to tell Millie the truth in that moment.

"I suppose that's true." Millie's eyes fluttered shut, her blinks becoming longer and more drawn out with each one.

"Listen." Jolene stood and walked over to Millie's bedside. She stroked her white hair. "I'm going to let you get your rest, but don't worry about a thing. I've got it all taken care of. Just try not to cause any trouble so they actually let you out tomorrow as promised. Can you do that for me?"

Rolling her eyes, Millie pursed her lips into a deep frown. "What's the fun in that?" she teased, then laughed the cutest little sound Jolene had ever heard.

Roger looked adoringly at Millie, an exchange Jolene caught.

"I'll see you both tomorrow," Jolene said. She squeezed Roger's hand before turning to go.

"We love you, Jojo," Roger called out as Jolene walked through the doorframe. "You know that, right?"

"Of course I do," she answered, grinning. "And I, you."

❄

JOLENE WASN'T EXPECTING to see the car in her driveway when she returned from the hospital later that evening, but she felt the tension in her shoulders slip away the instant it came into view. Pushing her foot down just a little harder on the gas pedal, she sped the last stretch of the way home, parking right behind Rose's black BMW.

She didn't even bother trying to keep it all in when Rose scurried down the walkway and threw her arms around her sister's neck. Jolene sobbed into the shoulder of her sister's puffy white coat.

"I'm so sorry, Jojo. After I hung up with you earlier, I got in the car and came straight here. I just couldn't bear the thought of you all by yourself with your sad, little breaking heart."

"When you put it that way, it sounds completely pathetic." Jolene straightened up and shook her head. "You didn't have to come all this way."

"Only took me two and a half hours. Hardly any time at all. It's amazing how much more relaxing it is to travel alone. No crying. No meltdowns. And that's just without Patrick!" Rose teased, poking playful fun at her husband.

"Well then, I'm glad my eventful day at least gave you the

opportunity for some peace and quiet. I really am happy you're here, sis. I need you right now."

"I know you do." Rose put her hands on either side of Jolene's face, scrunching down her fluffy curls under her palms. "Let's get you inside. I'll draw you a nice bubble bath, pour you a glass of wine, and we can share terrible breakup stories like we used to in college. It'll be a blast."

"That sounds awful. Well, the breakup story part. The bath and the wine sound amazing."

"How about we just say mean things about Luke, then? We'll make a list of all the reasons he never deserved you."

"That sad part is, I don't even want to do that. Deep down, I still believe he's a good guy, Rosie." Jolene felt the tears collecting again. "I want to believe that. Desperately."

"So do I, but all signs say otherwise."

"Just one sign," Jolene said. "One tall, beautiful, brunette sign."

"That's it!" Rose grabbed her sister's arm. "We're getting you inside. The wine is calling!"

22

LUKE

LUKE KNEW HE'D made a huge commotion, he just hoped Jolene wouldn't be able to hear it from within her house. Knowing her, she likely had holiday music blasting on repeat, drowning out any sounds other than those of holiday cheer. He was glad he'd reminded her to wear her warmest clothing, as the chill in the air continued to increase with each passing minute once the sun went down. Luke's hands had gone numb about a half an hour earlier, and he had little hope of regaining any feeling in them before the night was over.

Making sure he'd gathered everything he would need for their evening, he surveyed the dock one last time. Picnic basket. *Check*. Thermos full of hot cocoa. *Check*. Wool blanket. *Check*. His nerves. No checkmark there.

He'd rehearsed what he planned to say all afternoon, even reciting it once or twice in front of the mirror. Each time he fumbled over his words. He felt so stupid. He just hoped Jolene wouldn't pick up on his noticeable insecurity. Even if she did, he knew it was time to tell her how he really felt. He couldn't leave Merrylark without letting her know how she'd changed his life in just a few short days. It didn't even matter to him if she felt the same way, though he hoped she did. He owed her his honesty, whether or not that was returned.

When he couldn't procrastinate any longer, he set his plan into motion. Getting into the small aluminum boat proved more challenging than he had anticipated. Water sloshed at the sides, pitching the boat to the left when he lowered into it. Luke overcorrected, leaning his entire body to the right, trying to regain some balance. Luckily, the dock was still within arm's reach. Luke grabbed onto the wooden pier and steadied the rocking boat. Falling into Merrylark Lake on such a cold night would be awful. It would take him a solid week to thaw. With the lake house power still on the fritz, he'd have no place to warm himself. Staying in the boat was the only option. He didn't plan on swimming tonight.

Grabbing the oars, Luke made slow and steady work of backing the boat away from the pier. Moonlight reflected off the ripples in the water, creating long crescent shapes that echoed out from one another. Other than Luke's paddles that disturbed the surface, the lake was like glass. Before he made his way to Jolene's dock at the back of her house, he decided to spend some time alone on the water, really taking all of Merrylark in from this new perspective.

Each stroke of the paddle against the water pushed Luke further from the homes that lined the shore. Christmas bulbs strung on gutters became twinkling strands of tiny stars. His tree, all lit up and adorned, was the most beautiful sight to behold. For a moment, he stopped rowing and just admired it all. There was an element of magic that he'd felt the first time his boot planted on Merrylark soil, but this sight before him—this was that magic in visual form. He could see Mildred's home off to the right. The lights inside were turned on and he knew that even though Millie wasn't there, her cats were, and that someone—Jolene, he suspected—had taken great care to make sure the animals were tended to. Roger's home was on the opposite edge of the shoreline. He could make out the stacked firewood propped up against the side of the home and could see his old truck under a coating of snow in the driveway.

Then there was Jolene's house.

At first glance, it didn't look much different from the others. It had the same pitched roof and rows of lights outlining the windows and doors. But none of the other homes made Luke feel physically warm when he looked at them. Jolene's did. When he saw her house, he felt that same feeling that filled him the first night he stepped into it. She'd created an atmosphere of warmth that stuck with him. He had a feeling that this wasn't unique to Merrylark, after all. He suspected that anywhere Jolene went, that warmth and cheer would follow.

He knew in that instant, he couldn't go another day without it. Not even another moment.

Taking the oars in his grip again, he rowed quickly to her pier. His biceps burned with the effort and his lungs stung, but he continued rowing until the boat sidled up next to the dock. As he had suspected, someone had heard his earlier commotion when he'd overturned the boat from its resting place on the lake house deck. Standing at the edge of the pier, all bundled in a white quilted jacket was a woman, but it wasn't Jolene.

"Luke Handley," a familiar voice called out to him. Luke squinted in the dark, trying to make out the figure in front of him. "I suggest you turn that boat right around."

"Rose?" He shaded his brow with his hand, which was a silly thing to do at night. "Is that you?"

"If Jolene sees you out here...she'll...well, I don't know what she'll do, but it won't be good, I can promise you that."

Nothing Rose said made any sense to Luke.

"Can you send her out? She should be expecting me."

"Not a chance! After what you've done? You've got to be kidding me!"

"What have I done?" Luke was clueless.

"Oh, please. Now is not the time to play dumb, Luke. You've broken that woman's heart and I just spent the last hour trying to repair it. I *warned* you." Rose shook her finger at Luke from her place up on the pier. "Well, Patrick warned you, but I was the one behind that. Jolene has an entire town at the ready to go to bat for her, I'll have you know. That woman has sacrificed her time and her talents, always putting her friends first. There is not one person whose life she hasn't changed—"

"I know that, Rose," Luke interjected, beginning to get a little frustrated by the accusations she hurled at him. "She's changed me, too. That's what tonight is all about. I'm planning to tell her just how much she's changed me. How she's changed everything."

"The only thing you should plan to do is spin that boat around, hop in that old beat up, sad excuse for a truck of yours, and head back down the hill to wherever it is that you came from."

Luke was losing patience. "Rose, look, there seems to be some sort of misunderstanding. What you're saying isn't making any sense."

"Are you really that clueless, Luke? I have half a mind to tip you right out of that boat and into the lake in order to make you come to your senses! Is that what it takes?"

The step she took toward him made Luke think it wasn't an empty threat. He paddled back a few strokes to gain some distance from Rose and her hot temper.

"You've done some irreparable damage here and I'm not about to let you do any more. As far as I'm concerned, your lake house reservation is canceled. I expect you to be gone by morning."

Luke's head spun. He couldn't tell if it was the incessant rocking of the boat that made him suddenly nauseous, but he felt bile rising in his throat. How had everything changed since this afternoon? When he'd left Jolene, she'd been upset, but it wasn't with him. When he'd told her to wear her warmest winter gear for their evening together, he saw her face brighten with anticipation.

But suddenly here he was, ordered to leave Merrylark by sunrise.

"Rose, please. Can you just let me talk to her? I don't know where any of this is coming from. There has to be an explanation."

"I'm not going to let you charm your way out of this, Luke."

At that moment, Ace barked at the back door, two sharp and startling yelps. Rose looked over her shoulder.

"You need to leave, Luke. *Now*."

It wasn't a battle Luke was going to win. Rose's love for her sister was fierce and she was in full-on protective mode. Nothing Luke could say would change the way Rose saw things. Luke wondered if he should even bother trying. But to not challenge her was to give up, and that wasn't something he was willing to do. Not when it came to Jolene.

"Rose, please, just five minutes with her—"

Rose bent down and picked up an oar from the dock.

She took a leap forward and jabbed it at the rim of Luke's boat. The vessel wobbled violently.

"I warned you, Luke Handley!" She slapped the side of the boat again. "Don't test me or you'll end up at the bottom of Merrylark Lake!"

"Alright!" he shouted, then lowered his voice. "Alright. I'll go. But will you please tell Jolene I came by? Will you at least do that? I don't want her to think I forgot about our evening together."

"I think she thinks you've already forgotten about everything, Luke. Now she just needs to forget about you."

How could that be? Luke's head hurt from trying to process the sudden turn of events. But doing as told, he rowed his way back to the lake house. He wasn't quiet about pulling the boat up onto the dock this time. Anger fueled his movements. He threw the oars down on the wooden boards with a clatter. Twisting off the lid to his Thermos, he dumped the hot chocolate into the lake, watching it pour from the canister. It was wasteful, but somehow he felt better doing it. He gathered the blanket and basket and then stomped his way back up the pier.

The house was freezing inside, which didn't help his mood. He tossed a couple of logs into the fireplace and lit the kindling, frustrated when the flame took longer than he liked to ignite. After what felt like an eternity, a blaze roared to life. Luke crossed his legs on the floor directly in front of it. He stared into the flames, watching the white-hot glow change in colors from blue to orange.

How had things turned out this way? One moment he was ready to make plans to move to Merrylark for good, the next he was ordered to evacuate immediately. The thought of leaving on these terms made Luke physically ill. He couldn't leave without saying goodbye, but he knew he wouldn't have that chance, not if Rose had anything to do with it.

Everything felt so right this afternoon after talking with Kiara. She'd confirmed what Luke already knew—that he needed to tell Jolene he'd fallen in love with her. And just because Jolene suddenly didn't want anything to do with him, that didn't mean he could just shut off his feelings for her. If anything, it made them stronger. The thought of Jolene alone and brokenhearted only made Luke want to comfort her all the more. He just hated the fact that *he* was the one who somehow brought on that heartache.

Standing from the fire, Luke walked over to the tree in the middle of the room, taking in the memories, the stories, that night back when he'd wanted nothing more than to kiss Jolene and hold her in his arms. Now that would never happen. In reality, he might never even hear her voice again.

For the first time, Luke wished Roger would've just left him and Bessie on the mountainside, stranded and unable to make it up the hill. Maybe everyone—and everything—would've been better off if Luke had never come to Merry-lark at all.

23

JOLENE

AS WAS USUALLY the case, things didn't seem so bad in the morning. Of course there were those first few seconds right after waking to Ace's alarm-bark where Jolene had forgotten why her eyes were swollen and red, why her nose was stuffy and raw. But when the reality of what took place the day before came rushing back, all it took was an intentional, deep breath to keep the emotions at bay.

Luke wasn't the man she'd thought him to be. Oh well. Jolene would move on. When she reminded herself that just last week the name Luke Handley meant nothing more to her than a temporary next door tenant, things didn't seem so bad. All she had to do was mentally rewind her week back to when she didn't know he even existed. It wouldn't be that hard.

"Morning, sleepyhead," Rose said when Jolene shuffled into the kitchen in her pink robe and fuzzy slippers. "Or should I say bedhead? That is a serious rat's nest you're sporting there, sis."

Jolene opened the cupboard and reached for a red mug

that had the words *Silent Night* inscribed in white lettering on the side. "You know you're jealous. That perfectly straight, ready-to-wear hair can't be any fun to style. I like to start my day off with a challenge."

Rose laughed and took a sip of her coffee. "How'd you sleep?"

"Great, actually. I can't believe I crashed so early."

"You're worse than a toddler. You were out like a light practically before dinnertime!"

"I did wake up for an hour or so around midnight," Jolene said, shrugging. "A couple chapters of that science fiction novel I'm reading was all it took to get me to fall back asleep."

"Must be a riveting storyline," Rose teased.

"Oh, it is," Jolene answered sarcastically. "Sis, I feel awful that you came all this way to hang out with me and I left you alone last night. I didn't miss anything exciting, did I?"

"Nope," Rose said a little too quickly. "Not at all. This town really shuts down after dark, doesn't it? Like the entire population goes into hibernation mode. All was quiet on the home front." Rose shifted her eyes, avoiding contact with Jolene. "Anyway, Patrick called early this morning. Apparently Ava's got another ear infection. Won't stop crying and grabbing at her ear. I told him I'd head home as soon as you woke up, but I wanted to make sure things were okay here before I left you."

Jolene put her coffee mug on the counter so she could place her hands on her hips. "Seriously, Rose? Go home!" she scolded. "I'll be perfectly fine. Promise. Taking care of your daughter is much, much more important than anything I've got going on. You should've left already!"

"You're *both* important, Jojo," Rose emphasized. "You

were in a pretty bad way yesterday, sis. That Luke sure did a number on you."

Jolene felt sheepish when she admitted, "Is it bad that I kinda, sorta miss him already?"

"Please do not tell me you miss that lying, two-faced—"

"Okay, okay. I get it. He's not your favorite person."

"And he shouldn't be yours. He's not good enough for you, Jojo. Nowhere even close."

Too tired to argue, Jolene shrugged. She appreciated her sister more than she could express. But she couldn't switch off these feelings for Luke that had steadily grown over the last week. It would take time and a whole lot of *out of sight, out of mind.*

Rose left within the hour, kissing Jolene on the cheek and once again reminding her how valuable she was and how she deserved nothing but the best. Jolene believed her. She didn't deserve to have her heart broken; no one did. But that was the risk one took in letting others get close. When you opened yourself up to love, you also opened yourself up to pain.

After a long, hot shower, Jolene towel dried her hair and ran some peach lip gloss across her lips. She put on her favorite purple cable knit sweater, paired with black leggings and tugged on her fur-lined boots. Today was all about comfort. She had no plans other than curling up in front of the fireplace with a book and Ace. It was the perfect remedy.

She collected a book from her nightstand—this one a quick historical read—and padded out to the family room. She noticed Ace sitting by the narrow rectangular window flanking the front door. He didn't bark, but his attention was clearly fixed on something just outside.

"What is it, buddy?" Jolene asked, coming to his side. "Something out there?"

Opening the front door, Jolene's shoulders slumped. There, placed in the center of her *Welcome* mat, was a cardboard box, its flaps crisscrossed to keep the lid securely closed. Jolene bent down to pick it up. She didn't have to open it to know what was inside. When she stood up and looked outside, the bare, unembellished tree lying on its side on the curb next door made her heart feel like it bottomed out.

The driveway to the lake house was empty. The shades were drawn, just like they had been before Luke first arrived. The front stoop was shoveled and the snow dug out from the driveway. It looked vacant, completely empty.

"He's actually gone," Jolene whispered. Ace barked. "Didn't even say goodbye." Barking again, Ace let out a growl. "Oh, it's fine, boy. We'll be just fine."

Jolene told herself this would be good immersion therapy. She'd been afraid to be alone again. Well, now she would have to be. She'd be thrust right into the thick of it. She'd have no choice but to face her fears.

But she had expected a goodbye. A note, at the very least. But what would it have said? *Sorry, Jolene. I chose Kiara. Have a Merry Christmas and take care.* Any way Jolene spun it, a letter of the Dear John variety wouldn't help mend things. Maybe it was best that Luke left town unannounced. It would be a clean, quick ending.

Still, it all seemed so out of character. What Jolene knew of Luke was that he was an honest, sincere man who had gone through his share of sorrow when it came to relationships. That was why none of this made sense. His pain was still fresh; Jolene knew that. How could he turn around and inflict that same pain onto someone else?

"I'm not going to let this little hiccup ruin the holidays, Ace," Jolene said. She closed the front door a little harder than usual. "Christmas is about joy and hope and peace and Luke Handley will not take that away from us, right boy? We'll be okay. Promise."

Speaking the words out loud felt good, therapeutic even. Jolene could talk her way out of sadness—she'd been doing that for a long time now. So she went about her morning, narrating every thought and feeling and emotion to Ace, who didn't seem to mind one bit. He'd tilt his head where appropriate, wag his tail, or go in for a scratch behind the ears. His affection did wonders for Jolene's soul, always had.

It was nearing eleven when her ringing phone stole her attention away from washing the leftover breakfast dishes. She set down a freshly cleaned mug onto the counter and wiped her hands on a towel. When she picked up the phone, Jolene instantly recognized the number.

"Martha! How are you this beautiful morning?"

"Well, I've been better, dear." Martha sounded frazzled. Something clanged loudly in the background. "I seem to have lost my brain during this holiday rush and have more to bake than I have ovens available! I have a huge special order of candy cane shaped sugar cookies to deliver to the elementary school that I completely forgot about! Apparently, I'd promised them by this afternoon and all my ovens here are already full!" Martha paused, exasperated. "I know this is asking a lot, but I was reminded that you have two ovens and was hoping maybe—"

"You don't even need to ask, Martha. My kitchen is all yours."

"Really? You are a lifesaver, Jo!" Martha nearly screamed. "An absolute angel."

"I wouldn't go that far."

"I would! I'll be over within the hour, once I load up the truck with all the supplies. Would you mind preheating the ovens to 350 for me?"

"Already on it," Jolene said. She turned the dial on the oven and heard it beep in response. "Drive safe, Martha. See you in a bit."

❄

IF SNACKING ON Martha's sugary concoctions was the antidote to sadness, baking them took things to a whole new level of happiness. There was no possible way to be anything other than joyful when measuring out the sugar, the flour, the spices. Watching Martha in her element was like being on the set of a cooking show. She would swirl about the kitchen, dancing as she pulled sheets from the oven or flipped the switch on the mixer. It was all timed out perfectly, down to an edible science.

"I think if I worked at The Rolling Pin, I would gain about a hundred pounds," Jolene said, popping her finger in her mouth to lick off a sugary piece of dough. "Per month!"

"Why do you think they ask me and Gary to be Mr. and Mrs. Claus each year? Believe it or not, but I used to have an adorable little figure like yours. Twenty-five years' worth of sweets changed that just a little." She patted her round stomach with her palm.

Jolene thought back to the night of the tree lighting, when Luke had been so eager to whisper his wish into Santa's ear. She disliked the fact that every thought instantly went back to Luke. She had a lifetime of memories that didn't involve him, yet the ones that kept coming to mind were solely of him.

Slumping against the counter, Jolene took a spoon and

plunged it into the bowl of leftover cookie dough. "Do you ever get any strange wishes as Mrs. Claus?" she asked.

"Oh, sometimes. You know—the greedy little kid who asks for a Lamborghini or a mansion. But then there are the sweet ones who want world peace or for all the animals at the shelter to be adopted by Christmas." Martha's eyes twinkled. "And then there are the wishes about love. *Those* are my favorite."

"Love?" Jolene's heart caught. "What kinds of things do people wish for about love?"

"We'll get the romantic who's about to propose for the holidays and wishes for a *yes*. Or the one who's had a long-time crush and wishes for returned affection," Martha said. "But my favorites are the selfless ones. The wishes that don't benefit the wisher. The wishes made for someone else entirely and not for themselves." Martha put her hand on Jolene's arm and winked. "We had one of *those* ones recently."

Jolene knew who Martha was referring to. She didn't have the heart to tell her about Luke's recent bolt from town just yet.

"I think in all of my years of playing Mrs. Claus, that was my very favorite wish of all."

Even though she wanted to keep from asking, Jolene couldn't help herself. "And what exactly was that particular wish?"

Swatting her arm, Martha laughed. "You're not going to get that out of me, missy! Don't you know it won't come true if I tell? It's in our contract—sworn to secrecy." Martha made the hand motions of locking her lips tight with an imaginary key. She pretended to toss it over her shoulder.

Jolene wanted to say there was no chance of whatever

that wish had been coming true, anyway. Luke was gone and he took that wish with him when he left.

Suddenly, the timer chimed for the oven.

"Oh, goody!" Martha exclaimed. "I think we might actually get these down to the school in time! I don't know what I would've done without you, Jolene. You are a lifesaver."

"I'm so happy to help, Martha," Jolene replied. She smiled. "And grateful for the company." She looked at the large bowl of remaining ingredients on the counter. "Do you mind if I keep the extra dough?"

"Darling, if all you charge for your service is leftover cookie dough, you need to raise your prices."

"You know I'd help you even if the all-you-can-eat sweets weren't involved."

"I know you would," Martha answered and gave her friend a hug. "But it sure helps that they are."

❄

THE TIN WAS still warm in Jolene's hands when she grabbed it from the passenger seat. Stepping out of her car, she could hear the horses whinny from in their stalls and even though her heart rate picked up at the sound, she didn't feel as nervous as she had expected.

"Thomas!" Jolene called out when she got closer to the stable. "Brought you a little something. Freshly baked sugar cookies."

Thomas looked up, setting a grooming brush down next to Cyrpus's large hoof. "You brought me something?" He wiped his hands on his pants. "You're the one I should be bringing gifts to, Jolene. Or your boyfriend, at least. I don't know what I would've done without him the other night. He sure got me out of a real bind there. I know Cyprus is grateful."

Jolene whipped her head side to side. "He's not my boyfriend." She shoved her hands forward, giving the tin full of horseshoe-shaped cookies to Thomas. "And he left for home, anyway. He's not in town anymore."

"I'm sorry to hear that." Thomas took the cookies and tilted his head. "I do appreciate the cookies, Jolene."

Gathering her courage, Jolene took a breath. "It's not a completely selfless gift."

"No?"

"No." She twisted her hands together. "I was hoping I might be able to offer them as a sort of trade."

"A trade? For what?"

"I was just wondering if I could come by the barn every once in a while to spend time with the horses. Maybe learn more about them. Groom them. I'm happy to help muck stalls and things like that."

"And you want to *pay me* to let you do that?" Thomas grinned. "I think you've got things a little backward."

"I'll stay out of your hair. Promise. I just want to learn to be more comfortable around them and I think that will come if I spend more time with them. A friend once told me immersion therapy is a real thing."

Thomas put a palm on Jolene's shoulder. "Jolene, you are always welcome at the barn. I have to be honest with you, though. Even *I* feel out of my element here. This was definitely my dad's thing. I'm keeping the business going more out of obligation than true passion. Gosh, I feel like a horrible person for even admitting that."

"That doesn't make you a horrible person, Thomas. Just an honest one."

"Well, honestly, it will be nice to have someone around

the barn that knows even less than I do," Thomas joked. He reached toward the barn wall and picked up a rake that had a basket shape at the end. He handed it to Jolene. "Shall we start with scooping poop? That's one thing I actually *do* know how to do."

24

LUKE

L UKE SAT ON the edge of the bed, rubbing his hands, one over the other. He'd been home for only a few hours, but his heart was already set to leave again.

When he'd first pulled up to the ranch, his father, Curtis, was in the middle of trimming hooves, so Luke lent his hand. His dad had been in a mood to talk. Luke wasn't. He answered with grunts and nods, but offered no real information about his quick trip. His dad seemed content with that, picking up on the fact that Luke wasn't feeling exceptionally chatty. He'd always appreciated his father's ability to read Luke's emotions. They didn't talk in depth about much, but they had an unspoken understanding that Luke cherished.

Luke's mother, Patty, on the other hand, did not get the cue. Over lunch, she'd asked him about every detail of his trip, down to inquiring about the lake house bathroom décor and the number of stop signs in the small town. Truth was, Luke couldn't really remember any of those details. Merrylark Lake was all a blur.

What he could remember, though, was anything and everything pertaining to Jolene. The way her pale green eyes would lift at the corners when her cheeks pushed them up in a smile. The way her corkscrew hair would curl around her face and how his fingers ached to touch them, to feel their softness on his skin. The sound of her laugh. He still could hear it so clearly. How she could giggle and talk at the same time. He'd never met anyone who could do that before. It was like beautiful music.

But he didn't share any of that information with his mother.

He'd excused himself after their lunch. His apartment above the barn used to feel like home, but not anymore. Now it just felt like a barren bachelor pad. Glancing around the small space, Luke's shoulders sunk. There was nothing here that meant anything to him. It was just a box with a bed, a dresser and a small kitchenette in the corner. Nothing like Jolene's home where every aspect was meaningful and purposeful, filled with life and love.

Reaching for his phone, Luke dialed a number, figuring his call would go answered, but trying anyway.

"Handley, brother!" Devon exclaimed from the other end of the line, surprising Luke. "Didn't think I'd hear from you so soon. Rumor has it you left town in quite the rush."

"News sure travels quickly in Merrylark." Luke's stomach tensed at the thought of all of the possible stories flying around that little town to explain his swift and unexplained departure.

"Only because Jolene told Aunt Martha this morning."

"Jolene?" Luke's heart tripped at the mention of her name. "How is she?"

"Fine, I s'pose," Devon answered. "Gotta admit though, buddy—I'm a bit hurt you left without saying goodbye. I thought we were a good team, you and me."

"I know, Devon. I'm sorry about that. That's why I'm calling. I didn't really have much of a choice but to leave without any fanfare. I was more or less ordered out of town."

"Ordered? Who would order you out of town? You've been nothing but a blessing to us all."

"Jolene's sister."

"Didn't even know Rose was *in* town again. Well, whatever you did, must've been bad for Jolene's pint-sized sister to intimidate you enough to leave for good. She's a little bitty thing, if I remember."

"She sure is, but she was about ready to tip me out of my boat and into Merrylark Lake. Not something I wanted to experience."

Laughter roared through the receiver. "What in the world were you doing on a boat in the lake in the middle of December?"

Luke felt a sudden rush of humiliation sweep through him. He figured he didn't have any real reason to keep what he'd planned to do to himself, though, so he decided to open up to Devon. "In all honesty, I was going to tell Jolene I'd fallen in love with her." Luke waited for more laughter, but that didn't come. He continued. "I was going to take her out into the middle of the lake—into the very heart of Merrylark—to tell her that she'd become *my* heart. That I couldn't imagine my life without her in very center of it."

"So why on earth are you back in Kernlyville?" The tone of Devon's voice was like a wallop upside Luke's head. "Brother, that makes absolutely no sense whatsoever."

"I know. It doesn't. None of it does."

"So now what?"

Luke swallowed. "I have no idea. All I know is that I have to somehow tell Jolene how much she stills means to me, even if she won't let me say it. I have to get her to hear me."

"There *are* ways to let someone know you care about

them without using words. That's what we have to do here. We gotta find a way for you to *show* Jolene just what she means to you."

"A little hard to do when I'm over three hours away." Luke was defeated, no way around it, and even though Devon was trying to help, his suggestions felt like dead ends.

"So you need to come back."

Luke rubbed at the growing ache in his shoulders. "Where am I gonna stay, Devon? Certainly not the lake house. You know I love Merrylark, but it's definitely lacking in the hotel accommodations department."

"Good thing I've got a recently renovated studio apartment all set for you then."

Luke thought on it. It was a solid idea. The most solid one Luke had on the table, at least.

"I suppose that could work," he agreed, playing the idea out in his head. "But I'm telling you, Devon, I'm not liked in Merrylark. I wouldn't be surprised if Rose posted *Wanted* posters with my likeness on them all over Glenn Street. I won't be able to show my face."

"Haven't seen any yet," Devon teased. "But I'll keep an eye out."

"So what happens after I get there?"

"First things first, brother. Just get here. Tomorrow morning. We'll figure out the rest after that," Devon said. "But I gotta tell you, it would've been easier if you just called me before taking off so quickly. Would've saved you in gas money, at the very least."

"I know. I just kind of freaked out."

"Women will do that to us," Devon said, his laughter echoing through the phone. "Get a good night's sleep. I'll see you tomorrow."

※

LUKE'S GOODBYES WERE quick. While his mom was visibly disappointed that her son was leaving no sooner than he had arrived, Luke's dad understood that matters of the heart didn't adhere to any set timeline. Luke's uncle, Ted, was coming into town later that day to help out with the ranch, so the timing was ideal.

"Do what you need to do to make things right," his father had said when Luke loaded his truck up with a duffle bag and sleeping bag after an early breakfast of eggs and toast. Devon had a space available for Luke's stay, but Luke knew he didn't have the furnishings yet. He was fine with that. Crashing on the floor would be no problem.

"Thanks, Dad." Luke turned to give his father a hug, surprised when his dad held on for longer than usual.

"I mean it, Luke. If you really think she's the one, then do whatever you can to let her know. To make things work."

While the two had always been close, Luke's father was never one to share this sort of advice with his son, not even when Luke had talked to him about proposing to Kiara last year.

"But you haven't even met her."

"Don't need to. Just seeing you like this—broken hearted and at a loss as to what to do next—that's all the confirmation I need that she really means something to you."

Luke leaned his back against the side of his truck, folding his arms over his chest. "In fairness, isn't that pretty much the same state I was in after Kiara dumped me?"

"Not even close!" Luke's dad's voice lifted. He looked at his son thoughtfully. "I think that had more to do with the shock of it than anything. You and I both know that was a mismatch from the very beginning. I'm not grateful for the pain she caused you, son, but I am grateful things came to an end. Of course we would've welcomed her into the family, but she wasn't the type of woman I'd choose for my daughter-in-law."

"Jolene definitely is, Dad. She's amazing. Both you and Mom would love her."

"I don't doubt it." Curtis put his hand on his son's shoulder. "Things are going to work out for you, Luke. I have a strong feeling about this."

Luke wished he had his father's confidence. With each mile he drove in the direction of Merrylark, he felt his resolve slipping. Maybe this was stupid. It felt rash and spontaneous, but so did his decision to leave Merrylark. Luke was mid-thought, toying with the idea of giving Jolene the space she clearly wanted and leaving her alone forever, when the flashing lights reflected in his rear-view mirror seized his attention. He looked over his shoulder, only to see the officer gesture for him to pull off to the side of the road.

Luke groaned.

Rolling down his window after shutting off the engine, he looked up at the highway patrolman. "Morning, Officer."

The man tipped his head. "Morning. License and registration, please."

Reaching over to open the glove box, Luke retrieved the document for his vehicle. He remembered he'd placed his wallet in the front pocket of his coat though, rather than his back pants pocket so he wouldn't sit on it while he traveled. He pulled out his identification and passed it through the rolled down window.

"Thank you." The officer took the items from Luke and scanned them over. "You know why I pulled you over?"

Luke figured *head in the clouds* wasn't a specific reason, so he just shook his head.

"Left taillight's busted. Simple fix. I'm going to let you off with just a warning this time, but get that taken care of as soon as you can."

"I will. Right away. Thank you, sir."

"Where're you headed?"

"Merrylark," Luke replied. The officer held out the registration and I.D. for Luke to take back.

"Fantastic place. You been there before?"

"I have. Actually hoping to make a permanent move."

"Well, if that's your final destination, be sure to look up a man named Hank Haverstein. He'll get you all set up with a new taillight at a great price. I've run into him and his big tow truck many times out on this road. He's a great guy. The best."

Luke just laughed. "I'll look him up. Thank you again for being so understanding. I'll get it fixed right away."

The officer clamped his hand on the truck's driver's side window frame and gave it a pat. "Take care and Merry Christmas to you."

"Same to you."

After the officer left, Luke stayed pulled over on the shoulder for a few extra moments. He couldn't ask any more favors of Hank. Luckily, fixing a broken taillight was well within Luke's car mechanic repertoire. Bessie was sure showing her age lately, but Luke didn't mind tending to her. Chuckling, he wondered if she'd be the only girl in his life from here on out.

Reaching over the passenger seat, Luke placed his registration back into the glove box. Then he slipped his hand into his jacket pocket to put his driver's license back into his leather wallet. It was then that his fingers grazed across something made of paper, folded in half and tucked deep into the fabric pocket. Taking it in his grip, he slid it out from his jacket.

Kiara's letter.

He hadn't bothered reading it yet. Whatever was written in it couldn't at all be life altering. Still, curiosity got the best of him and Luke found himself slipping his finger under the sealed edge to see what was inside. He lifted the flap. He'd expected to see pages and pages of Kiara's cursive writing, but there was just one sheet of paper inside. A check. Luke looked at the sum and his mouth fell open in shock.

$30,000.

Luke had never seen so many zeroes, one after the other, all on the same line.

Peeling a sticky note from the check, he read Kiara's words.

Luke:

I know all the money in the world cannot pay for the damage I've caused between us. Even still, this is my only way to truly make things right. I was able to convince the caterer, the photographer and all of the rental companies to give us back our deposits. And even though you wouldn't accept the ring when I tried to give that back to you last summer, my hope is that you will take the money for it instead. This money belongs to you—for you to build your future upon. I know you will make it a beautiful one.

With love always,
Kiara

25

JOLENE

"IT'S ALL QUEUED up and ready to go. Just push play." Jolene tucked the wool blanket under Millie's feet and handed her the remote. "Anything else I can get you?"

"A handsome young man to fan me with palm fronds and feed me grapes." Millie tugged roughly at the blanket as she situated herself on the sofa. She jabbed Roger with her elbow. "This old geezer will just snore throughout the whole movie and drool on my shoulder, too. Does every dang time."

"She's probably right about that," Roger admitted, shrugging. "Even more likely after staying at the hospital last night. They don't seem to know the difference between night and day there. I'm lucky if I got three hours of shuteye with nurses popping in every hour or so to take Millie's vitals and check up on her."

"And I got even less with all of your gargling and wheezing!"

Jolene looked at her friends and smiled. Based on Mildred's quick and prickly remarks, Jolene knew she was feeling one-hundred percent back to her old self.

"Just call me if you need anything. I'm around all day."

"We'll be fine, dear," Roger said. "Go about your day. I'll take care of my Millie. Don't you worry about us one bit."

Before leaving, Jolene made sure all the cats had full water and food dishes. She even placed an extra bowl outside on the front porch, just in case Ozzy wasn't the one they'd buried out back. One could always hold out hope.

It was a beautiful day. The air was crisp, the snow crunchy, and puffy white clouds hung high in the sky like bunches of cotton candy suspended in a blanket of blue. As she drove to the barn, she took time to appreciate the clarity this new day provided. The brief storm had passed. She knew it was more than just a metaphor and wouldn't take that for granted. Life was good.

"Jolene!" Thomas hollered as soon as she stepped from her car. He raced toward her, his strides clipped and fast. "Glad you got here when you did. I've got to leave to check on Dad and the horses still need feeding. Would you mind giving them their lunch? A flake of hay each in their stalls."

"Oh, goodness. Is your dad okay?"

"He'll be fine. Just a bit out of sorts today. More than usual, I guess. I'd just feel better if I could spend the afternoon with him. It feels like the barn takes up all of my time and attention these days and I know my mom struggles to care for Dad all on her own."

"I'm more than happy to help with anything you need around here, Thomas. Just name it and I'll do it."

Jolene surprised even herself at the offer. She'd have to overcome her horse fear quickly. There were just some things that required you to suck it up and get the job done. Taking care of a friend definitely met that requirement.

After Thomas left, Jolene walked over to the hay storage, an open front gambrel roof barn with red siding and white trim. Bales upon bales were stacked ten feet high. She found an empty laundry basket and filled it with grass hay to carry over to the stables. As though she'd rung a dinner bell, Cyprus and Clara whinnied boisterously at the sight of Jolene with their meal. Jolene could hear them pawing at their stall doors, their locks jostling and clanging as their hooves pounded against the plywood.

"Alright, alright," Jolene said once she got closer to the animals. "Hold your horses." The joke was a tired one, but it didn't keep her from bursting into laughter. "I'm sure you get that all the time, right?" As though he could understand every word, Cyprus's head bobbed up and down in answer. "Yeah? What else? Why the long face? That's a classic." Unlocking the door to Clara's stall, Jolene hesitantly walked in, careful to keep a wide berth. She dumped the hay into a large green tub and then backed away. Clara seemed more interested in the hay than in Jolene, and for that, Jolene was immensely appreciative.

"Not so bad," she muttered to herself as she locked the horse securely in. "Okay, big boy. You're next. Lunch time!"

Jolene unlatched Cyprus's stall door, but unlike Clara, he didn't move to allow her through.

"I'm going to need more room than that, Cyprus." Jolene balanced the basket on her hip. "Back up."

Cyprus took one step back. Jolene cocked her head. "Did you do that because I asked you to? You really are a smart boy, aren't you? Okay. Let's see if you can do that again. Back up."

One more step.

"Wow," she breathed. "That's amazing. It's like you understand what I'm saying. Go on now. Back up."

Another step.

"You are one special horse, aren't you?" If she'd felt

comfortable doing so, this would be the place where Jolene would scratch his ear or pat his big cheek. But she wasn't about to touch him. She would continue to appreciate him from a safe and secure distance.

Jolene dropped the remaining hay into the tub on the ground. "There you go. Eat up, buddy."

Unlike when she'd asked him to back up, Cyprus didn't lower his head to eat. Instead, he glanced down at the green hay and then back up to Jolene.

"Eat up," she tried again. "Remember? Like back up? Only eating instead of backing."

Cyprus took another backward step but bumped into the stall wall, startling him and terrifying Jolene. Faster than she could say Merry Christmas, she bolted out of the stall, swung around, and slammed shut the door, locking it into place.

"I guess I sort of told you to do that," Jolene admitted, out of breath. "Go on now. Eat your lunch."

Ignoring the food, Cyprus came over to the door and stretched his long neck over. Jolene shrugged backward, away from the intimidating animal. From where she stood, she could feel his warmth on her face, and when he blew a sputtering breath out from his mouth, she about jumped out of her skin.

"Cyprus, you have to eat. Thomas gave me one job and so far only half of it is completed. Clara's doing her part— your turn to do the rest. Eat your hay."

The two stared at one another, a stand-off in the barn.

"Not going to give in, huh? Well, I've got an idea." Jolene raised her index finger in the air. "Wait right there. Not that you're going anywhere, really."

Hurrying to her car, she retrieved her brown sack lunch she'd packed earlier that morning. When she came back,

Cyprus was in the same position, his head stretched out of the barn stall, ignoring the meal waiting for him.

"You just want some company, don't you, big guy?"

Jolene reached into the bag and pulled out a ham sandwich. She took a bite. "See? I'm eating my lunch. Clara is eating her lunch. We're *all* eating lunch. Lunch time!"

Cyprus didn't budge.

"Oh, come on, boy. You're going to make this difficult on me, aren't you?"

Like earlier, Cyprus nodded. Jolene was beginning to think the horse was a descendent of Mr. Ed.

"Fine then. Back up." She ordered him backward until there was enough room to safely enter the stall. "Okay. You win." She held up her sandwich and took a bite, overly dramatic in her movements. "*Now* eat your lunch."

Surprising her, Cyprus bent his head down to snatch a mouthful of hay from the tub. He raised back up and crunched loudly.

"I'm the horse whisperer," Jolene said to herself, amazed at her newfound ability. "You just wanted a lunch date, huh? Well, funny thing—I'm actually on the market again. Not sure if you remember that guy who worked all the magic on your hoof, but he and I kinda, sorta had a thing going. I thought we did, at least. But that's over. He left Merrylark yesterday. Not sure if I'll ever see him again, actually." Jolene lifted her sandwich to her mouth, pausing. "Wow. It's pretty sad when I say it out loud like that. I mean, in fairness, I hardly knew him all that long. But maybe you don't have to know someone long to know they're everything you've been missing in your life. Luke sure felt like that missing puzzle piece in my life, even if it was just for a short while."

Cyprus continued snacking on his hay, but he'd look up

at all the right places and to Jolene, it really felt like someone was listening.

But that might've had more to do with the fact that Thomas was standing just on the other side of the stall door.

"Thomas!" Jolene screamed, throwing her sandwich across the barn. It hit Thomas directly in the face. "Oh my gosh! I'm so sorry! How long have you been standing there?"

"Only a minute." He swiped at a streak of mustard on his chin with his thumb. "I forgot to tell you that Cyprus sometimes likes company for his meals, but I see you've already figured that out."

The heat of humiliation crept up Jolene's neck. "How much of my rambling did you hear?"

"Don't worry. Your secret is safe with me, Jolene, although I don't think it's much of a secret. Anyone who spent any amount of time with the two of you could easily see just how much you both cared for one another."

Hearing things like that wouldn't help Jolene get over Luke any faster. Instead, it served only to further confuse her. "Luke was just a neighbor," Jolene lied. "Nothing more. Anyway, he's gone and I'm here and I think from here on out I'll just be content with my singleness. Plus, now I've got all this extra time to hang out with the horses."

"I know they appreciate it. And so do I," Thomas said. "Enjoy your lunch, Jolene."

"We will," Jolene answered, followed by Cyprus's whinny of agreement. "Horse whisperer," she quietly said to herself. "I like the sound of that."

26

LUKE

L UKE WONDERED IF it would feel like being inside a cave, but to his surprise, it wasn't that way at all. Having all of the windows covered with brown paper to keep anyone on the outside from seeing in felt like being wrapped inside a Christmas present, a surprise about to be uncovered. Luke had been back in town for three days and though he'd had to keep his stay a secret, it turned out to be easier than he'd expected.

The most difficult part, he'd found, was knowing how close in proximity he was to Jolene without actually being able to be with her, or even see her. The thought of Jolene strolling on the sidewalk just outside the store made Luke want to throw open the door and race to her, sweeping her up in his arms and telling her right then and there how much she still meant to him.

He couldn't do that, even though he dreamt of it every minute of the day.

"Cat's on her way over," Devon called over the buzz of the handheld drill. He set the tool down and slammed his hand on the counter to test the durability of the butcher block tabletop screwed into place. "Man. That looks good, no?"

"Looks incredible," Luke agreed. He swung around the counter's side to stand across from Devon. "Afternoon, sir. Can I take your order?"

"Just a plain ol' cup of joe for me."

"Still doesn't sound like the right name for this place, does it? Too generic."

Devon nodded. "I agree. Give it time. It'll come to you."

"I hope I'm doing the right thing here, Devon. What if all of this backfires on me?"

"It won't, brother. I promise you. Every single person we've talked to has been nothing but utterly impressed with our stroke of storefront genius."

"The only person I really want to impress is Jolene."

"She will be impressed. No doubt about it." Devon took Luke's shoulders into his grip and looked him in the eye. "You need to just trust me on this."

"Knock, knock!" The front door popped open a sliver, enough for Luke to see Cat's black-lined eye peering through. "Safe to come in?"

"Yep! Come on in." Devon waved her inside, shutting the door behind her and locking it quickly.

"Vick's parked out back. He and Tanner will unload the machine and bring it in through there if that's okay. Not too many places in town to hide that big ol' beast of a truck."

"That's the perfect spot for it. I'll go out to meet them right now," Devon said. He unhooked his tool belt and placed it onto the counter.

Luke followed Cat's gaze around the room. He tried to read her expression, but it was blank and untelling, giving nothing away.

"Luke," she mouthed, her voice soft as a whisper, not

something he'd ever expected out of Cat. He figured she only had one volume: full blast. "I have no words."

"Is that a good speechless or a bad speechless?"

"It's a *holy guacamole, I cannot believe what you two have created here* speechless!" She laughed, tossing her head back with a cackle. "Well, would ya' look at that—found my words. Knew that wouldn't last long."

"You still think this is the right thing to do? You don't think I'm making a huge mistake here? What if she hates it?"

"It's the *only* thing to do. Ever since you and Devon gathered us all to tell us about your plan, it's all I can think about. I just wish we could speed up the build out process. I know you two are busting your buns to get some of Martha's baked buns in here, but it's the hardest thing I've ever had to do to lie to Jojo. Today I had to tell her I sold the coffee truck to a Swedish trapeze artist based out of a San Antonio circus! It's absolutely awful keeping the truth from her!"

Luke's brow knit together. "Why such an elaborate lie?"

"You *have* seen my truck, haven't you? Painted magenta with a big ol' fat cat drawn onto the side? You should know everything I do is over-the-top elaborate, even my lying!"

"I appreciate you keeping this a secret, Cat. Shouldn't be more than a couple days at this point. We're pretty much just waiting for the paint to dry," Luke said. "That and the permits to come in."

"Vick knows quite a few people down at the county. I'll see if we can pull some strings. If they're like anyone else in Merrylark, their lives have been touched by Jolene's in one way or another, too. Once they hear what you're doing for her, those permits will get signed right off. I have no doubt about it."

"Coming through! Wide load!" Devon's voice rung out from the backroom. He shuffled in doing the moonwalk, holding one end of the espresso maker, Vick at the other end. Tanner walked next to them, making waving motions with his arms that resembled someone attempting to land a plane.

"Right over here, guys." Cat rushed to the counter just as the trio settled the machine onto the newly installed tabletop. "Perfect fit."

"And with that, you officially have yourself a coffee shop, Luke Handley." Devon came up behind Luke and slapped a palm between his shoulder blades. "Congratulations. This really is just what this town needs. Aunt Martha will have a space for all of her extra bakery items, the town will have a place to relax and hang out, and Cat will be free of that monstrous, gas-guzzling coffee truck. It's a win-win all the way around."

Luke couldn't say he wasn't pleased with the way things had turned out. It was remarkable how quickly he and Devon had been able to transform the once empty space into an inviting retreat. The furniture was exactly right. The decorations were spot on. Every detail was absolute perfection.

"It really does feel like Jolene's, doesn't it?" Cat remarked. She spun on her heel to survey the room again. "All we're missing is, well, Jolene!"

"And a name. Cup of Joe just doesn't feel right anymore now that it's finished," Luke admitted.

"I agree with you on that. Feels too generic and Jolene is anything but that," Cat said. "So let's think back to the first time you set foot in Jolene's home. That's what we want to recreate here—the feeling of coming home. What emotion did you feel in that exact moment, Luke? Can you remember?"

That was an easy answer. "Joy. Cheer," Luke said. He

paused, thinking. "I'd have to say cheer. With all the Christmas decorations and her kind invitation to stay for a cup of coffee—what I felt was completely full of holiday cheer."

"Well then." Cat winked at Luke with her thick false lashes. "I'd say you've got yourself a name."

"Cup of Cheer," Luke said, loving the sound of it.

"Cup of Cheer." Cat nodded. "It's perfect. Just like our Jolene."

❋

LUKE HADN'T BEEN able to sleep a wink. The fact that he was crashing on a blowup mattress in a box of a room had little to do with it. Even if he'd been slumbering in a plush bed fit for a king in a castle, he knew sleep wouldn't've come. He just had too much on his mind and too many butterflies swarming in his stomach. It was as though their constant flutter kept waking him each time he'd start to drift off, a tap-tap-tapping reminder that his nerves were taking over.

At half past two, he decided to give in to the insomnia.

He pulled out a pair of slippers from within his duffle bag and walked down the stairs to the new coffee shop just beneath the studio apartment. The lights were out and with the windows covered, the space was pitch black. Luke flipped on a lamp next to the corduroy couch and sat down.

Though he and his friends had meticulously attempted to recreate Jolene's family room in the space, he knew without Jolene in it, it would never feel complete. It had been a rush of hard work and emotion, but every detail was finally put into place and the big reveal scheduled for later that day.

It worried Luke that he didn't know what he'd get. Based on his interaction with Rose, Luke figured Jolene never wanted to see him again. If that was her desire, it would have to be okay with Luke. Ultimately, he wasn't doing this for himself. He was doing this entirely for Jolene.

He knew her heart for this town. He knew her wish to be an even bigger part of it. And he knew that her years of sacrificing for her friends ultimately led to the sacrifice of realizing her own dream.

Kiara had said to use the money from their cancelled wedding to build out Luke's dreams and future. If he'd learned anything from his short time with Jolene, it was that a life lived for others was infinitely more rewarding than one lived only for oneself.

It was time to put into practice the lesson Jolene had selflessly taught Luke during his week at Merrylark Lake.

❄

HE MUST'VE FALLEN asleep on the couch sometime in the wee hours of the morning, because just around sunrise, Luke felt a nudge against his shoulder, an attempt to rouse him from sleep.

"Is sleeping in just not a thing in Merrylark?" Luke grumbled, rubbing at his eyes. He smacked his mouth and yawned.

"Big day, brother," Devon answered, holding out a mug for Luke to take. "Gotta get you sufficiently caffeinated!"

Luke sat up and took the cup. He looked into it. "Nice job with the latte art. A snowman?"

"Supposed to be a wolverine, actually, but snowman works."

Luke laughed. He sat back against the couch and sighed.

"I'm not sure I can go through with this today. I'm even more nervous than when I proposed to Kiara, and I just about lost my lunch over that."

"You have *nothing* to be nervous about. You have met Jolene, haven't you? She has to be the nicest person to walk the earth. And even if she doesn't like it, the worst thing out of her mouth would be something along the lines of, 'This just isn't my favorite.'"

"I think *I'm* not her favorite."

"Maybe not right now, but once she sees what you've done for her here, you'll shoot straight to favorite-person-ever status."

Luke took a swig of the coffee. "Honestly, none of that even matters to me anymore. I just want her to be happy, even if that means it's not with me."

"Spoken like a man that is absolutely head over heels in love." Devon glanced at Luke's feet. "Or head over slippers, I should say. Listen, brother, go on upstairs. Take a long, hot shower. Clear your head. Cat and I will get everything ready here. Aunt Martha's coming over in an hour and Roger and Millie shouldn't be too long after that."

"I can't tell you enough what your help and friendship means to me, Devon. The fact that you were willing to take a chance on my crazy idea means more than you know."

"In fairness, it's not really taking a chance at all. The fact that Jolene will be running the shop makes it a sure bet. Everyone loves that woman. And Aunt Martha's day-old pastries are just the icing on the cake." Devon took the coffee cup from Luke's hand and placed it on the low table in front of them. "Go on. Get yourself cleaned up. *Please.* You say you only care about Jolene's happiness, but you should also care a little about your friend's ability to breathe. Because right now you are pretty ripe, brother. Pretty ripe."

"Okay, okay. I get the hint. See you in a few." Luke stood to go. "I really hope we can pull off this surprise, Devon."

"I know we can," Devon replied, utterly confident. "And it might not be the only one this town will get today, either."

27

JOLENE

J OLENE NEVER LIKED when her friends called her in a panic. It seemed like that was happening more and more these days. From Millie's sudden fall to Martha's overbooked oven snafu, Jolene's friends were consistently getting themselves into pickles of all kinds.

It wasn't that Jolene minded being called upon for help. She actually loved that her friends felt like they could count on her in a time of need. It was the desperation in their voices that she disliked. She never liked the thought of the ones she loved in distress.

So when Martha rang her again that morning while Jolene was out at the barn, her voice full of unease, Jolene took on those same emotions. She couldn't help but be empathetic when the people she cared about were in a bind.

Martha had said Devon ran into an issue at his new property. Something about an application for a permit being denied. Jolene wasn't sure how she'd be of any help in the situation, but she was glad to offer whatever assistance she could. Martha said the county officer knew of Jolene back from college and that at this point, whatever connections they could make would greatly increase their chances of the permit coming through.

Of course Jolene was eager to lend her hand, but she'd be lying if she said she wasn't equally as interested in learning a little more about the plans for the storefront. When she saw the brown paper coverings go up in the windows earlier in the week, admittedly, her curiosity had been piqued. She was also just a touch saddened, knowing the ideas she and Luke had discussed back at The Rolling Pin would never come to fruition in that location. Even still, it would be good to fill the vacant space on Glenn Street. Merrylark would benefit from the addition of a new business, and for that, Jolene couldn't be more pleased.

She found a parking spot just outside the store, almost like it had been reserved for her. She couldn't believe her luck. Downtown Merrylark was absolutely bustling these days. With each day closer to Christmas, the sidewalks seemed to increase with shoppers by the dozens. Just as she pulled the keys out of the ignition, Jolene saw Martha burst out of the entrance door, slamming it shut behind her. She looked out of breath and beyond distraught, her hair all wayward and her apron twisted across her body.

"Jolene, dear!" She scurried over to Jolene's driver's side door, grabbing the handle to help her open it as though Jolene wasn't moving quickly enough for her liking. "You're finally here!"

"Morning, Martha." Jolene stood from her vehicle. She wrapped Martha in a hug. "Like I said on the phone, I'm not sure what help I can be, but I'm happy to offer it."

"Of course. Of course," Martha spoke over Jolene's words in a rush. She took her by the hand like a mom taking hold of a child. "Right this way. Right this way."

Jolene's feet planted on the curb. "Are you okay, Martha?

You seem a little out of sorts. Maybe you should stop and take a breath. Should I be worried about you?"

"No, no. I'm just fine. Just fine. Concerned that permit won't come through, that's all."

"Do you mind me asking what type of establishment Devon plans to put in here? That might be good information to have before I meet the officer from the county," Jolene suggested. Something just didn't feel right about Martha's level of both distraught worry and visible eagerness to get Jolene into the building.

Martha gave Jolene's hand a firm squeeze. "I think it's better if I show you, rather than tell you."

Dragging her forward, Martha pulled Jolene across the pavement and up to the door. She looked over at Jolene. "Maybe close your eyes first."

"Close my eyes?" This was all sounding suspicious to Jolene. "Martha, why would I need to close my eyes?"

"Because it's an absolute mess inside. Pigsty."

"And closing my eyes will help with that how?"

"I'm not sure. It just feels like the right thing to do." Martha was reaching, clearly. "I'll close mine, too." She slapped her free palm over her face. Not knowing why, Jolene followed her lead and did the same. "One...two...three!"

Martha dropped Jolene's hand and tugged the door open by its handle.

Jolene half expected to be greeted with the roaring shout of the word *Surprise!* but even though that didn't occur, it didn't lessen the shock that fell over her the moment the inside of the shop came into view.

At first she couldn't take in the space in it's entirety. What she did see, however, were the beaming faces of her dearest friends. Roger stood immediately in front of her, his frail arm draped over Mildred's shoulders. He smiled so brightly Jolene saw reflective tears welling in his eyes. And next to Roger and Millie was Gary, a tray of coffee cup shaped cookies in his hands, all lined up and iced to look like red mugs with dollops of whipped cream on top. To the left of Gary was Ivy. Her smile shone so brightly and she clasped her hands in front of her like she was trying hard to hold in her excitement. Next to Ivy was Devon. His eyes connected with Jolene's and he tipped his chin in a courteous nod. Thomas stood behind him. He shot Jolene a quick wave. Her cousins Hank and Tilly were in the back row, holding up a phone with the image of her sister, Rose, waving on the screen. Cat and Tanner and Vick stood up front and they had their arms linked together, hugging one another to their sides.

Jolene could see Travis, her mailman. There was her hair dresser, Georgia, and her dog groomer, Edwardo. In fact, there were too many people to name. It would've been easier for Jolene to list those who *weren't* there than to name those in attendance.

Cat slipped her arm out from her husband's and walked over to Jolene. She smiled at her dear friend, her bright red lips lifting in a massive grin.

"Welcome to your new home away from home, Jolene."

"Mine?"

On cue, the crowd parted.

Jolene looked around the room. She could see a near replica of her couch, the Christmas throw pillows resembling the same ones she had propped up on her sofa back at the house. There was an evergreen colored arm chair that looked just like the one she had next to her fireplace in her family room. The holiday décor was so similar to what she'd used at her house that she felt as though she'd just stepped through her very own lake house doors. It was cozy and inviting and held a sense of familiarity that immediately made the space feel like it belonged to her.

"This is all for you, Jojo," Cat explained, her smile never wavering. She took Jolene's trembling hands into her own. "For years, you've given to us. To every single one of us in this room and even to many who aren't here. But now it's your turn to be on the receiving end of a little generosity. It's no secret that you've wanted a place of your own here on Glenn Street. And you could've had that years ago if you hadn't put everyone else first, time and time again. But that's not who you are, and I know that I, for one, am immensely grateful for your selfless, giving, and caring nature, Jolene. You are our town's biggest blessing. Now it's our turn to bless you."

Jolene couldn't keep her bottom lip from trembling, even when she pinned it between her teeth. Her eyes clouded and she blinked several times in a row to keep from crying the happiest tears she'd ever had. She inhaled deeply, filling her lungs.

"I don't know what to say." She glanced around the room, surveying every inch of it. "All of you did this just for me?"

"All of us did a little," Cat answered. Then, looking over her shoulder she said, "But one of us did a whole heck of a lot."

Stepping forward from the back of the shop, Luke came into view.

Jolene's heart all but stopped.

Luke wore his infamous cowboy boots, dark denim jeans, and a black sport coat that made him look so sharp and unquestionably handsome. Hesitantly, as though he didn't know if he should, he edged his way through the gathering of Merrylarkers toward Jolene. He stopped right in front of her with the same wary and endearing smile he wore the first night they'd met on her front porch.

"Hi," he said softly. Jolene could detect the quiver in his voice, and she knew that if she dared to speak in that moment, that hers would match exactly. "Jolene," he started after clearing his throat. He closed his eyes briefly as though needing a moment to collect himself. "Jolene, I came to Merrylark to take a break from my life. I called it a sabbatical." He glanced over his shoulder toward Devon and smiled. "Others called it a respite. Whatever you label it, in my mind, it was a chance to press the pause button on what my life had become at that time."

With hesitancy in his eyes, he looked down at Jolene's hands, as if he were asking her permission to hold them. Reading his uncertainty, Jolene took the lead and grabbed onto his. Immediately, Luke's entire demeanor changed. He confidently gathered his breath and continued.

"What I learned this last week is that I wasn't hitting the pause button because that would mean going back to that old life once I finally pushed play again. I don't want to go back to that life, Jolene. I want to start completely over, here with you." He swallowed. "But I know that somehow I've hurt you, and there aren't enough words in the English language to say how sorry I am for that. If there's one thing I've learned in my thirty-two years, though, it's that actions will always speak louder than words. So I hope what we've created here speaks to you in some way. I hope that when you look around this place, you hear it as one big *thank you* from every single person in this room."

Luke's hands shook within Jolene's grip. She squeezed them to steady him and looked into Luke's eyes expectantly.

"And I hope that in addition to those *thank you's*, you

also hear my *I love you*. Because I do, Jolene. I love you. I never thought I could meet someone and so quickly know I wanted to spend every moment—every last breath—with them. But that's what you've done to me, Jolene. You've made the thought of a life without you feel so much less than one with you in it."

"But what about Kiara?" Jolene asked, opening her mouth for the first time since Luke began talking.

"Kiara?"

"I saw the two of you the other day at Sal's, Luke. At lunchtime."

"You saw us?" Luke's forehead tensed.

"Kissing."

Like he'd been hit by a Mack truck, Luke stepped backward. "That kiss? That wasn't supposed to happen, Jolene. Kiara kissed me as a goodbye, I guess. I would never willingly kiss her; you have to know that."

Deep down, she did know that. In a way, Jolene supposed her rash and sudden anger toward Luke was her attempt to protect her heart. If she cut him out of her life first, then he wouldn't have the chance to cut her out. It was her defense mechanism, even if it was grossly unfair.

But now here they were, standing in front of the other, the huge misunderstanding that had been wedged between them for the last few days suddenly lifted.

Jolene felt like she could breathe again.

"I love you—and *only* you—Jolene. And I'll love only you even if that love isn't returned," Luke said. "I will completely understand if after this you want nothing to do with me. I get it. But I couldn't live with myself if I knew I could do something to make a dream of yours become a reality, yet did nothing about it."

Jolene gasped, utterly stunned.

"I was told by someone recently to make my own dreams come true, but the only dream I have is one that revolves around your happiness."

"I don't know what to say, Luke," Jolene said through tears that streamed down her cheeks. "I'm completely overwhelmed."

She was overwhelmed by his actions, amazed by his words. But his character—that was what captivated her the most. She'd said before that Luke was one of the good ones, and this show of humility was just further confirmation of what her heart already knew to be true.

She was in love with Luke Handley, even more than she ever thought possible. And it was time she let him know.

"I love you, too, Luke. Even when I thought this journey we'd started together was over, I didn't stop loving you. I couldn't stop." Throwing her arms around his neck, Jolene stood up on her toes to draw herself closer. "I love you, too."

Luke pulled her close to his body. He pressed his chin to the crown of her hair, breathing in deeply.

"Jolene?" he said, his voice rising on the syllables. "Why do you smell like a horse?"

Laughter burst from between Jolene's lips. "Because I've spent the last three days hanging out with my new best friend, Cyprus."

Turning around, Luke made eye contact with Thomas. Thomas just nodded, grinning ear to ear.

"Seriously? You've become a barn girl in the short amount of time I was gone?"

"In fairness, you've become a coffee shop owner, so I suppose we've both been a little busy creating alternate identities."

"No." Luke shook his head side to side. "This place belongs completely to you. It's all yours."

"What if I don't want it to be all mine? What if I want a business partner?"

Stepping forward, Martha cleared her throat. "Well, that's actually good to hear, because you've got yourself quite a few partners already. Gary and I will be supplying all of the baked goods you could ever need, Ivy's got a line of knit coffee cup koozies she's planning to offer here, and Cat will be in charge of all things coffee-bean-business related. You know what that leaves for you?"

Jolene shook her head.

"Cheer," Martha answered.

"Cheer?"

"Of course. Since the shop is aptly named *Cup of Cheer* and all."

Jolene's eyes widened, awe rounding them. "I couldn't love it more!" she exclaimed. She squeezed Luke tightly within her arms. "And I couldn't love you more. You've made me the happiest girl in Merrylark, Luke Handley."

Hugging her, Luke looked down at Jolene, his mouth spreading into a slow, knowing smile. Then his lips met hers, softly and tenderly as his eyes fluttered closed. Luke leaned in closer, deepening their kiss and holding onto Jolene like she was his lifeline, his love, his everything.

Hoots and hollers bellowed around, continuing even when they pulled apart.

Jolene didn't mind the attention one bit. She jumped up into Luke's arms and planted another kiss firmly onto his lips. Roars of applause filled the room, everyone rejoicing in their friends' much deserved happy ending.

"Any chance we could get some actual coffee at this coffee house?" Devon interjected, his voice a shout over the joyous celebration.

Luke grabbed onto Jolene's waist and lowered her gently

onto the floor. "Let me do it! I've actually been practicing this."

Racing over to the espresso bar, Luke slid behind the counter. Jolene giggled as she watched him tie the apron around his neck and over his sport coat, rub his hands briskly together, and grab a mug from on top of the machine. Luke adjusted the buttons and the espresso machine hissed to life. Steam rose in curly billows, the scent of rich coffee infiltrating the room.

Jolene loved every bit of it. After he'd finished brewing his coffee creation, Luke passed the cup toward Jolene across the counter, pride worn visibly on his face.

Peering into the mug, Jolene glimpsed Luke's latest latte foam art. It was by far his best one to date.

"A heart?" she exclaimed. "It's perfect, Luke. Absolutely perfect."

"Only for you," he said, taking an elaborate bow. Then he waved his hand across the room. "The rest of you get snowmen."

"Or wolverines," Devon shouted. "I can draw a mean wolverine."

Jolene took a sip and held it in her mouth. It warmed every inch of her and was hands-down the best cup of coffee she'd ever had. But it was more than just a cup full of coffee. It was a perfectly crafted cup full of cheer.

ONE YEAR LATER

LUKE AND JOLENE

LUKE BLEW ACROSS the lid of the cardboard box. Dust particles scattered into the air like bits of glitter, catching the morning light that streamed through the coffee shop windows. The shop wasn't set to open for another hour and Luke figured now was the perfect time to trim the tree before the morning rush.

"Can you believe it's already that time of year again?" Jolene walked across the store, carrying two coffee mugs in her hands. She settled one down onto the table and handed Luke the other. "Doesn't it seem like just yesterday we were decorating your tree at the O'Connell place?" she reminisced. "I'm sure glad they chose not to sell and decided to move back to the lake instead. Turns out, they're pretty awesome neighbors! And Ace just loves his Lucy. He can't get enough of that fancy poodle of theirs!"

"I think it's fair to say we can expect a litter of furry mutts come springtime," Luke teased. Setting the cup of coffee down, he lifted the box's lid and smiled at Jolene. He reached inside. "Tell me about this one."

"Oh, are we doing that again?" Jolene took the ornament

from his hand. She turned it over in her palm. "Okay, so this one was given to me by my old running partner, Trista, after a half marathon we completed three years ago to benefit childhood cancer research. Hence the yellow tennis shoe."

"Gotcha. And this one?"

"Ah, the toothbrush ornament. That's from my dentist."

"The infamous flamingo!" Luke said excitedly. He held up the sparkling ornament by its hook. "In fairness, I don't think you're actually as clumsy as your sister and mom claim you are. Just a little coordinationally challenged, that's all."

"So that mishap last week when I spilled the entire bag of sweeteners on the floor and then proceeded to trip on them, landing on my backside—that went completely unnoticed, huh?"

"No, I noticed. But I'm giving you a pass on that."

"How kind of you," Jolene said. "Oh, Luke. I've forgotten just how much I love decorating for the holidays."

"How could you forget? Christmas is your favorite."

Jolene shrugged. "I don't know. Honestly, every season this last year with you has been my favorite."

Luke walked over to Jolene and swung his arms around her, planting a kiss on her lips and bending her backward like a dip in a dance move. They righted themselves and Jolene lifted up to place a quick peck on his cheek.

"Back to decorating," she instructed, swatting at his chest to push him away. "We don't have long until I have to open for the day. We need to deck the halls!"

Jolene hung the flamingo ornament on one of the higher branches and stood back to see if it was the right location for it. She always liked her decorations to be evenly spaced out among the branches. When she spun back around to collect another ornament from the box, Luke was down on his knee, a red ribbon threaded through a diamond ring held out on his index finger.

"What about this one?" he said, his voice cracking.

Jolene's mouth fell open.

"Jolene, one of the greatest memories I have is when we decorated my tree last year. How we spent the entire evening reminiscing about all of the ornaments you'd been gifted by your family and friends, and how you shared the memories attached to each one."

Jolene could feel her eyes welling, her chest tight with anticipation. She brought her hands to her gaping mouth and held them there.

"My hope is that today we can create the most beautiful memory to date. Better than the sum of all of the memories held in that box." Luke reached up to ask for Jolene's shaking left hand. She lowered it into his. "Jolene Carter, will you do me the absolute honor of becoming my wife? Will you be my memory making partner for the rest of our days?"

Jolene bounced up and down, unable to keep from celebrating. "Of course!" she proclaimed. "Of course I will, Luke. Yes. Yes!"

Jumping to his feet, Luke pushed his lips to Jolene's and grabbed her into a huge bear hug.

"Do I get to wear it?" she stammered. "Or do we have to hang it on the tree?"

"You absolutely get to wear it," Luke said, sliding the ribbon from the ring and placing the solitaire diamond onto Jolene's fourth finger. It was a perfect fit.

"How long have you had this planned, Luke Handley?"

"Since last Christmas."

Jolene's eyes widened.

"Of course I knew I had to wait, but there was no question in my mind that I would one day ask you to be my wife. Oh!" He held up a finger. "Wait right there. I forgot one thing."

Jolene couldn't make a guess as to what this next surprise could be. She waited anxiously as Luke rushed to the backroom. When he returned, his hands were cupped one over the other.

"These were delivered a few days ago and I'm not sure what do to with them since they are just too beautiful to throw away, so I was hoping maybe you might have an idea as to what we could use them for." Luke opened his hands to reveal several dozen red rose petals just like he had the night they'd met.

"Luke. They're beautiful." Taking a few in her fingers, Jolene tossed them into the air.

Luke threw the remaining rose petals up between them, and they trickled down slowly, landing in their hair and on their clothes.

"You certainly are quite the romantic. Who knew?" Jolene kissed Luke on the lips. Then, realizing the time, she said, "You have to get going! Devon should be here any minute!"

As if on cue, a horn bellowed a blaring *ahooga!* just outside the coffee shop doors. Devon waved at his friends through the passenger side window of the massive truck, which had once been home to Cat's Coffee Cart. Now it boasted the words *Handley and Manning Handyman Services* across the broad exterior length of it.

Not long after Luke's big coffee house reveal, Devon surprised Luke with a secret project of his own. Unbeknownst to Luke, Devon had repurposed the ailing truck with the hopes of using it as a work vehicle for his new business with his friend. Over the course of the last year, the two had repaired boats, installed cabinetry and flooring, land-scaped lawns, and even did a little farrier work at the Silent Night Stables. Their schedules were constantly booked and Luke found he loved nothing more than helping his Merrylark neighbors.

Luke was living his dream job. In fact, he was living his dream life. And now he would have Jolene forever by his side to live it out with him.

"Looks like duty calls." Luke lifted Jolene's hand to his mouth and kissed the back of it. "I'll see you after work, *fiancé*."

"Oooh, I like the sound of that!" Jolene said, beaming.

Luke gave Jolene one last hug and then collected his canvas jacket and scarf from the coat rack near the coffee shop's door.

"Wait! Don't forget Ozzy!' Spinning on her heel, Jolene snatched up the overweight orange tabby from his cozy bed underneath the tree. "He'll be so mad if you forget to take him to work with you again."

As it turned out, Ozzy hadn't at all been run over back when he'd slipped out Millie's front door on that fateful day last winter. In fact, they soon discovered Ozzy made a daily habit of sneaking out of Millie's place and onto Cat's Coffee Cart when it came through the neighborhood. It could've been the free *cat*-uccinos that Cat fed him or it could've been the alluring draw of the feline of similar likeness painted onto the side of the truck that kept him coming back for more, but Ozzy had turned out to be a more adventurous cat than any of them had realized.

His new favorite activity involved accompanying Luke and Devon on their house calls. He'd become their unofficial handyman mascot, much to Mildred's chagrin. No cat of hers would be caught gallivanting across town, drinking fancy coffees and sleeping in once food trucks. That was likely the reason she was so quick to offer Ozzy to Luke and Jolene. They'd grown to love the quirky cat, so it was a win-win all around.

Scooping the fluff ball from Jolene's arms, Luke turned to go.

"Don't work too late. Tonight's the annual tree lighting and I want to make sure we don't miss it this time," she teased.

"Devon and I plan to take off early after we help Thomas get the horses ready for their big sleigh ride. Don't worry. I don't want to miss my chance to make another Christmas wish, either. I'll be back in plenty of time."

Remembering back to the year before, Jolene said, "You never did tell me what you wished for."

"You really want to know? After all this time?"

Jolene nodded. It had been something she thought back to often throughout the last year.

"I wished that you would get to live a life where you felt cherished and loved by a man that was truly worthy of you. I wished that I could become that man, but even if I couldn't, that you would still find him. Because all that matters to me is your happiness, Jolene." He leaned in to kiss her on the forehead. Ozzy meowed, sandwiched between their two bodies. "Always."

"Looks like that wish definitely came true. So what wish do you plan to make tonight?"

"I'm not sure yet. I'll have to think about it. All of my wishes seem to be coming true these days. Not sure I could ever wish for anything more than what I've got right here, with you."

"How about a white Christmas?" Jolene suggested. "I

know you've always wanted to experience one of those. That would be magical."

"You are all the Merrylark magic I will ever need, Jolene," Luke said before propping the door open to join Devon out in the truck. "I hope you know that."

She did, and she celebrated the fact that the two would spend the rest of their lives in Merrylark Lake, making magic together.

❄

THE END

ABOUT THE AUTHOR

Growing up with only a lizard for a pet, Megan now makes up for it by caring for the nearly forty animals on her twelve-acre flower farm in Northern California. A UC Davis graduate, Megan worked in the political non-profit realm prior to becoming a stay-at-home mom. She then spent nearly ten years as an award winning photographer, with her work published in magazines such as Professional Photographer and Click.

In 2012, her creativity took a turn when she wrote and published her first young adult novel. Megan is both traditionally and self-published and *A Lake House Holiday* is her eighth publication. She can't go a day without Jesus, her family and farm animals, and a large McDonald's Diet Coke.

To keep up with Megan online, please visit:

 facebook.com/MeganSquiresAuthor

twitter.com/MeganSquires